Palaces of Sin,
or,
The Devil in Society

Also from Westphalia Press
westphaliapress.org

Palaces of Sin,
or,
The Devil in Society

by Col. Dick Maple

WESTPHALIA PRESS
An Imprint of Policy Studies Organization

Westphalia Press
An imprint of Policy Studies Organization
1527 New Hampshire Ave., NW
Washington, D.C. 20036
info@ipsonet.org

ISBN-13: 978-1-63391-605-0
ISBN-10: 1-63391-605-7

Cover design by Jeffrey Barnes:
jbarnesbook.design

Daniel Gutierrez-Sandoval, Executive Director
PSO and Westphalia Press

Updated material and comments on this edition
can be found at the Westphalia Press website:
www.westphaliapress.org

Yours Very Truly
Dick Maple.

"PALACES OF SIN"

...OR..

"The Devil in Society"

The Crimson Hand of Society Exposed.

The Painted Cheek of this Fashionable "Hag" Smote by the Hand of Justice.

The Black History of Harlotism in "High Life" Painted in Letters of Fire.

A History of "Society's Sins" that Appall the Civilized World.

Written by a man who spent his fortune with lavish hand, but awoke from his hypnotic debauch of Society's shame, to wave the red flag of warning to his fellowman.

A book which should be read by every mother and father in the land, and placed in the hands of their sons and daughters as a guide to their young feet.

By

Col. Dick Maple,

Who spent nearly a million dollars in "Society's march to Hell."

Published by
National Book Concern,
St. Louis, Mo.

Author's Announcement

In placing this volume in the hands of the reading public, I do so after years of deliberation, as I endeavored to ease my conscience by trying to force myself to believe that I had performed my duty, in tearing myself away from "Fashionable Society" and endeavoring to live an honorable life, but there were many who had heard me talk upon the subject of "Fashionable Society," and many are the mothers and fathers who have, with tears in their eyes, begged me in the name of humanity and as a protection to the young men and young women of this country to write a book vividly portraying the rotten condition of what the world calls "The best" or "The Fashionable Society" of this country.

I hesitated a number of years, but the more I hesitated the more thoroughly I became convinced that it was my duty to place a book of this kind in the hands of the reading pubic, as I had never found a book of this character upon the market.

It is easily explained why no one has ever written a book similar to this, as those who are in this seething abominable cauldron of shame are too busily engaged in their giddy whirl to destruction to pay any attention to the welfare of humanity, and but few who have ever entered this cyclonic whirlwind of social dissipation ever emerge from its blighting influence with sufficient manhood and womanhood left to correctly and vividly portray the scenes of their degradation, therefore, the indulgent and ignorant fathers and mothers of this land allow their sons and daughters to be dragged down to lives of shame by not being prepared to warn them of their sure fate, should "Fashionable Society" lay her ungodly hands upon their innocent offspring.

I have received hundreds of letters from mothers and fathers who have heard me lecture upon the subject of society's depravity, but still I rebelled at the idea of sending broadcast through the land a volume that would brand myself as being once a dupe and follower of this immoral herd of degenerates, but the longer I procrastinated the keener conscience pricked me on the account of my unwillingness to perform my duty; therefore, this volume is placed in your hands, by the entreaties of fathers and mothers, who are interested in behalf of, not only their own sons and daughters, but in behalf of innocent and inexperienced manhood and womanhood throughout the land.

Reader, I am ashamed of the life that I lived for a number of years, but, thank God, that I had the manhood to extricate myself from Society's abominations and place my feet once more upon the solid foundation of morality which is the fundamental principle of pure manhood and womanhood the world over.

I have been saved from the awful abyss of "Fashionable Society," which has led more men and women down to a disgraceful and premature grave than any other one thing this world has ever seen, not excepting that awful "Red-eyed Demon," Rum, as rum is the main corner stone and prop of society, therefore, it naturally becomes a part thereof, consequently when we speak of "Fashionable Society" we include "Rum."

Believing that this book will be read by the young and rising generations, and knowing that if they will give its contents due weight they will stand aloof from the contaminating influences of "Fashionable Society." Such being the case, I will feel that I have

[7]

been repaid ten thousand times for this very embarrassing task which forced me to openly acknowledge that I was once covered with the filth of "Fashionable Society."

Yours very truly,

DICK MAPLE.

List of Illustrations.

Table of Contents.

(11)

Table of Contents—Continued.

(12)

"COL. DICK MAPLE" – His first entry into Fashionable Society after falling heir to his Aunt's money.

Chapter I.

My First Sight of Washington Society.

Col. Henry Watterson, editor of that great paper, "The Louisville Courier-Journal," has made himself famous in many ways, one in particular was by delivering a great lecture entitled "MEN AND MORALS," or "MONEY AND MORALS," which, we have almost forgotten, as it has been quite awhile since we had the pleasure of hearing this most famous man deliver this lecture. However, we think it should have been upon the subject of "MONEY AND FOOLS," as we have a larger class this lecture would exactly fit, myself in particular.

A "natural fool" is a sad thing to behold, but a "self-made fool" is still more sad, and this is the class that I belong to. It might be by a "tight squeeze" I could be entered in the "natural fool" ring, but, of course, I would not acknowledge this.

"A fool" is not necessarily a man or a woman who has no natural intellect, as an individual of this class would be termed an "idiot" who is wholly irresponsible and who is to be pitied, however the "natural born fool" is not to be pitied near so much as the fool who is "self made," and we have a larger number of 'self made fools" than we have of "natural" ones.

One reason why I know I am a "self made fool" is from my past actions, for at an early age in life a very rich relative of mine died and left me a "snug" fortune, which I came in possession of when I reached the age of twenty-one, and as soon as possible I proceeded to "blow" the hard earned cash, hoarded up by this dear old relative, who was a good old soul, with the exception of being a "self made fool" as she thought more of a dollar than she did of her prospects of eternal bliss. As soon as I came into possession of my Aunt's money I proceeded at once to "edge up to society," as I thought it was the "proper thing," I being a "fool," and I continued being a fool until over three-fourths of my money was gone, when I awoke with a start, and realized that "fashionable society" was the most hideous "Hag" mortal man ever beheld. MONEY! Oh! the good thou hast done, and the lives thou hast wrecked!!

While I had money I moved in "all "kinds" of society and I beheld "all kinds" of sights which I will endeavor to relate before I am through with my task, and if the reader has a few thousand dollars he desires to use in demonstrating to his friends that he or she is a "self made fool" he can see the same sights, behold the same gorgeous hosiery, look upon the same female shoulders, naked almost to the fourteenth or fifteenth joint of the vertebra, commonly called the backbone, and how far down in front I would not dare say, neither could I, as there is no backbone to measure by, but if you have the money and care to make a "fool" of yourself, you can go into "Society" (?) and behold all of the above, and in addition to this you will be permitted to breathe the sweet aroma of "Cigarettes" puffed by "Ladies" (?) or at least they are "Ladies" as far as "Society" is concerned, or until their idiotic old "Dad" "spills his milk," then society "cuts" this dear creature with the "gorgeous socks and bare backbone," and allows her to "drift"; but remember she "drifts" in exactly the same direction she was drifting when she extravagantly displayed her gorgeous "socks" and

(2)

the upper part of her anatomy, only she "drifts" faster as her course is not impeded by the lavish expenditure of money by her old "Sap-headed" father. But if you have money and the desire, you can move in the "Best of Society" (?) and see all of these things, yea, and more too, as the sights referred to are only the "side shows" before you enter the main tent where the Elephants are and the "bare back riders" perform. Decency, you know, is not essential to any one who has money and belongs to "swell society."

Yes, if you have money you can get right up against the "Best society" (?) and sit under its eave and get your very soul begrimed with the soot of contamination, which nothing but God can wash off, and He must not let you alone very long if He expects to make a good job of it.

I remember very distinctly the first "real swell" society gathering I ever attended after coming into posssssion of my relative's money. Now, don't think that it was the very first, for I had been initiated in small towns up in Indiana, such as Lampyra, Vilgreene, Radford and others too numerous to mention. Then I spread out to Louisville, Ky., as I had too much money to stay in small towns, and from there floated into Philadelphia, Boston and New York.

But, as I said before, "the real thing" happened when I arrived at Washington, D. C., and the daily papers announced next morning that "Col. Dick Maple, of Indiana," the talented Hoosier millionaire, had arrived in Washington, and proposed spending some time in the Capital. This article stated that I had fallen heir to $9,000,000.00, and was spending it with a lavish hand, and dilated upon my being one of the best fellows of the age.

You can imagine my surprise when this article was pointed out to me by a reporter from a leading journal in Washington, who called that morning and asked an interview. I told him certainly. Now, reader, if you can imagine my feelings, you will have to drink about four quarts of "Hard cider" and take two tablespoons full of common soda, as I indeed felt windy.

The reporter asked my plans while in the Capital, and I informed him that I expected to remain in Washington indefinitely, and further let him know that I was out for a good time, and did not give a red cent what it cost, as I had more money than forty men could count in a century if it was all in hundred dollar bills, and the forty men all experts, and convinced him of the truthfulness of this statement by handing him a thousand dollar bill, and gave him to understand that I wanted every move of mine to ap pear in print, and had him send two other reporters from two other leading Washington papers, which I treated in like manner, therefore, I was the most talked of man in Washington, and at least four hundred scheming old mothers began to set traps to catch the "Rich Hoosier" for their daughters, and you can rest assured that I was well looked after.

The third day I was at the Capitol, I received an invitation from Mrs. Middlewest, the wife of an official from the State of Missouri, asking the great honor and pleasure of my presence, on the next Wednesday evening, to a party in honor of her daughter, Clara's, eighteenth birthday.

I, of course, accepted the invitation and arrayed myself in the barbaric costume of society, which made me feel like you or any other man feels when he breaks a suspender in company, that is, you feel like you need help.

I drove to the residence of Mrs. Middlewest on "F" street, alighted and passed my card to the man at the door dressed up like an organ grinder's monkey. Imagine my great delight when Mrs. Middlewest rushed down the broad marble stairs with outstretched hands, and a smile upon the front part of her head that resembled a gash in Mt. Pelee's side, and on reaching me she made a "squat" that society calls a bow, and in a flow of language which sounded like the soft murmur of water escaping from a "bath tub" begged to be permitted to introduce me to her daughter, Clara, in whose honor this party was given, stating that Clara was the dearest "thing" on earth.

Clara came, and I was introduced to the dear "thing," and not a womanly woman. She was dressed in some kind of a sort of soft "Muliky Mulk." I mean the lower part of her was clad in this garment, with short sleeves and a very short bodice, that exposed six or seven ribs.

Such a sight I had never seen before; in fact, I did not know whether I was intended to look at it or not, and when I had to look toward her I sorter "squinted" with one eye, believing that it was my duty to do so.

In a few moments, however, I was convinced that "Society," I mean the "real thing," in Washington, D. C., was a "naked truth," as about eighteen other "backbones" appeared, consequently I concluded that I could risk both eyes.

But hold on! We have only started with Mrs. Middlewest's party, and the "Hot Time" is yet to come, as this party was "IT" with all the trimmings, in fact, the society papers of Washington stated that it was one of the "swellest" social affairs that had ever been "pulled off" at the Capital.

We had music, dancing, jigs, cake walks, in fact, there was almost everything done imaginable, and to the shame of mankind.

About 12 o'clock we had supper; after supper came wine and champagne in abundance, and to my utter surprise all of the "Ladies" (?) without one exception, drank wine and champagne like veterans. Not only one glass, but many, many glasses, and, you know, that many, many glasses not only loosen the tongue, but it loosens character, and within two hours I could accurately give the color of every pair of stockings in the audience.

Not only the young and giddy were under the influence of liquor, but the old "fat jawed" matrons, who were trapping for a husband for their daughters, would talk as though they had "bunions" on their tongues, and would at times feel so "giddy" that they would be inclined to fool with their feet in an extravagant manner, thereby giving the audience a chance to behold their "socks."

At this gathering were represented what society is pleased to call the best people in the land, as the progeny of the politicians from all over the country were there, and not only the progeny, but the Politicians themselves, and their wives, who were good, well meaning, common, industrious people until the political bee struck the family, and by a lucky whirl of the wheel of fortune, they were landed at Washington, where society does not care a fig for honor or virtue, just so you have money and can entertain and "Monkey" and "Ape" after some sort of "nobility" whose parents have lived upon the fertility of their wits, and who never earned an honest dollar in their lives.

But we are getting away from the subject of Mrs. Middlewest's party, and the horrible part of the story relative to this party is yet to come, for two hours of drinking wine and champagne does not satisfy Washington society, as they can not get their hides full enough of liquor in that time to show off their depravity to the best advantage.

As yet I have mentioned only the girls and their mothers, but this chapter would be incomplete, not to mention the "Simple Simons" dressed in men's clothes, and the old "Touts," who call themselves "Aristocrats" and the lawmakers of the land, as both classes of this biped race of "leeches" were there, and they were "drunk" also, for you can not call it anything else, but a "plain drunk" of both men and women, who claim the right to set the example for you and me and our families, and should we undertake to give such a debauch at our homes, our neighbors would have us arrested as a "nuisance," and we would be compelled to change our abode, as we would not be considered decent, and the judgment of our neighbors would be upheld by any honorable court of morals.

Well, the more wine and champagne that disappeared down the depraved "guggles" of this gang of "Society pirates," the more boisterous became their actions, and the greater was the desire of the females to display their "socks," and the more anxious was the male contingent to behold the same.

What? Who was that asked what I was doing? Well, to tell the truth, I had my hands full in trying to keep Miss Clara and her mother off of my anatomy, as it seemed as though they had prearranged to at once bridle and ride "bare backed" rather than allow me to get away, as they considered a man worth $9,000,000.00 worth getting; however, I lacked about $8,000,000.00 of having that amount, but I did not try to correct the error, as I was anxious to have "The gang" believe me a regular forty-acre lot in the heart of the "Klondike," as I was a "fool," you know.

I acknowledge that I had drank considerable wine and champagne; however, I had been more discreet than the others, as I did not propose to make a "mess" of myself, the first time I broke into the "Bull Pen" of society in Washington; therefore, I was prepared to carefully observe the actions of this tribe of prospective "Hoboes" and "Hoboesses," for the fate of such a lot is as certain as that of the "Prodigal son."

About three o'clock in the morning the younger element began to waltz, both men and women, actually being so full of "booze" that they did not know whether they were waltzing or dodging an angry bull in a peach orchard; however, they continued this crazy whirl with such rapidity that the ladies' dresses would swing out from their person so far that it seemed to me that decency was unknown in that audience of what Washington called "elegant society."

At the close of each of these idiotic scenes, the older ones (fathers and mothers) would clap their hands in drunken approval, while old Mrs. Middlewest would "hunch up the furnace of passion" with a few more "slugs" of wine and champagne.

About half-past four o'clock the audience was actually so drunk that it was an absolute necessity to bring this grand function to a close; therefore the carriages were called, and to my certain knowledge seven out of the eighteen ladies (?) had to be walked between two gentlemen to their carriages to keep them from falling in a drunken sprawl.

Clara, dear "thing" was so "stinking drunk" that she had to retire before all the ladies left the house, but, be it said to Clara's great credit (?) that she could stand up under a load of liquor that would make a sea captain turn green with envy.

A number of the ladies (?) had to be bodily picked up and placed in their carriages, as they were so "full" they could not have seen a total eclipse of the sun.

Now, reader, this is the class of degenerates that presume to set the pace for your family and mine to pattern after, however, of course, they do not expect for the general public to learn of their society debauches.

I bade good-night to Mrs. Middlewest, and she endeavored to impress me with the idea that the party would have been a failure had I not been there; however, she had drank about seventeen too many glasses of "Hell's populator," and her mutterings reminded me of the melancholy lamentation of a mule's "Grandma."

Well, "my first jag in Washington society" had passed into history, and had left me many times wiser, but I frankly tell you that I was also many degrees lower in the scale of morality, as I felt as though I had disgraced the name of "Maple" by being any part of such a "society drunk," as that was all it was in plain English.

Within the next few days I had received fourteen invitations to parties, given by that many old scheming mothers, as they could not get the reporter's tale of $9,000,000.00 out of their old "soft pates," and each was dead bent on catching "it" for their daughter.

Well, I had the bad luck of meeting Clara, the dear "thing," many times within the next few weeks, and each time I met her, and she had half a chance, she would invariably get her "kite out," as she loved

wine and champagne better than the healthiest kind
of a "Jersey Calf" likes its native beverage, consequently, she would always proceed to fill herself with
a quantity that would make her feel as though the
earth was not good enough for her feet, therefore,
handled them as though they were built for the
purpose of navigating the air.

Clara, and Clara's mother, seemed determined to
have me understand that I was to become one of
their family, as they tried in every conceivable manner to impress all they knew with the idea that
"Col. Maple" had already proposed and had been accepted; however, I never missed an opportunity to
let both of them know that I was not "on the market" and had no desire to become the husband of a
"Female distillery" and the son-in-law of a "She lob-
ster."

All at once, Clara, the dear "thing," ceased to
show her "hosiery" at the social functions, and I
could not imagine why it was thus, unless she had
broken one of her lower limbs in trying to get her
foot upon the top of the "White House," however, I
did not feel that it was just the right thing for me
to make inquiries about her, for fear that "Society"
might begin to think I was unduly anxious about the

dear "thing" and arrive at the conclus'on that perhaps the tales Clara and her mother had been telling about my having proposed were true. Therefore,
I concluded the best thing for me to do was to keep
my mouth shut, and listen, as I frankly tell you, I
was interested in the girl to a certain extent, for she
was not a bad looking girl, and had been a bright,
lady-like country girl before her father had entered
politics and sold his family for the emoluments of a
small office, which had turned the head of his wife,
and sunken the ladyhood of Clara deep down in the
grime of drink.

Party after party, and excursion after excursion
would come off, but neither Clara nor Clara's mother
would be seen, and the queer part of the matter was,
no one ever mentioned Clara, neither did they ever
mention Mrs. Middlewest, consequently, my curiosity
kept growing until I began to wonder if I was actually in love with her, or was I losing my mind. However, one evening while being entertained by the very
popular Mrs. Bigmouth, an official's wife, from the
State of Illinois, and who, by the way, had a daughter, who also needed a husband with money, I
chanced to mention the name of Miss Clara Rushford
of Indiana, who was visiting her uncle in Washing-

ton, and made the remark that she was a very elegant lady.

Immediately Dorothy, the daughter of Mrs. Bigmouth, asked me if it was Miss Rushford that I was
so well pleased with, or was it simply the name
"Clara?" I at once saw a chance to make an inquiry
about Miss Clara Middlewest, so I asked what had
become of Miss Clara, stating that I had not seen
her for some time.

At once, both the old and young "tittered" behind
their fans, trying to impress me that they were so
modest they could not even look at a man who would
ask such a question.

I, of course, had sense enough to let the subject
drop, as I' did not know, but what she had gotten
"drunk" and had been "run in." In fact, I could not
surmise what had become of her, but this "titter-
ing" sharpened my curiosity, and I was determined
to find out what had become of Clara Middlewest at
!all hazards, if I had to call upon her mother and
ask "point blank" where she was.

I acknowledge that I did not enjoy Mrs. Bigmouth's party, as the whole thing was a "farce" and
not natural at all, for the guests all had their clothes
on "clean up to their chins," and not a drop of liquor

in sight, and the same "gang" was there (excepting
Clara and her mother), as were at Mrs. Middlewest's
party, and I knew that it was not natural for that
"lay out" to act as they were, but the secret of this,
lay in the fact that Mrs. Bigmouth had learned that I
utterly detested these "Social Drunks" and also much
preferred "ladies" with all their clothes on, therefore her cunning wits suggested the idea of playing
the part of "modesty" and "temperance," believing
she would be better able to favorably impress the
"Hoosier" with her daughter.

Well, I had been raised by good Scotch parents,
who had taught me that

"The truth itself was not believed

From one who often had deceived,"
therefore, I concluded that I was "on" to their "self-
righteousness."

The party came to a close about eleven o'clock, as
there was not one present who could keep awake and
carry on an intelligent conversation, so the party had
to be closed for the lack of "talk," as that "gang"
could not "talk" without first getting on the outside
of at least two pints each of wine or champagne,
and then their talk sounded like a drove of Filipino
monkeys; however, it was "talk," and gave the 'La-

dies" a chance to unblushingly display to the male
sex their utter depravity.

But where had Clara Middlewest gone? This was
the subject that most interested me. Find out I
must. I was not left in ignorance long, as Mrs. Bigmouth soon gave me the desired information. Her
carriage halted in front of my hotel one brisk, chilly
morning, and her "flunkey" brought up her card
stating that she would be pleased to speak to "Col.
Maple."

I "puckered" myself up, just as any other fool
would do, and rushed down to see what the dear
"old thing" wanted. She informed me that she had
stopped in order to have me take a ride with her
that "very delightful maw-ning," stating that she had
some news for me. I, of course, accepted her invitation and crawled in beside her, and she must have
had four gallons of different kinds of musks and co-
lognes sprinkled upon her "harness," as it was a
closed carriage, and the aroma reminded me of the
perfume of a basket of wet pups.

We had not gone far until she turned to me and
said: "My Dear Colonel." Bear in mind, reader, that
the title "Colonel" never attached itself to my anatomy until I came into possession of my Aunt's
money.

As stated above, she says, "My Dear Colonel" and nestled up to me as though she would like to put her hands in my pocket, and with a look in her eyes that resembled "six bits" said, "You know you asked my daughter a short time since what had become of Miss Clara Middlewest." I said "Yes, I have an idle curiosity to know where this very charming lady has gone," at which old Mrs. Bigmouth heaved a sigh that sounded like escaping gas from a sewer pipe, and said, "Colonel, I am married, and a lady." I says, Yes, I know you are married," then I coughed and never 'd finish my sentence. "Therefore," says she, "I feel that I can talk to you upon this subject with propriety, while my dear innocent daughter could not, therefore, I have invited you to take this drive with me that we may be all alone so that I could tell you all about Clara Middlewest and her troubles."

I acknowledge that I became somewhat nervous, and anxious to know what had befallen Clara and asked Mrs. Bigmouth if she had broken a leg, which seemed to quite flustrate the "old thing," and she gave me a look that would "sour goat's milk."

I apologized to her in a "Hoosier" way by telling her that I was glad it was not her leg, which
(3)

seemed to square me with her. Then she began by saying "Colonel, you know that Miss Clara was a green country girl, and had never been used to the 'ins and outs' of society, therefore, you know, Colonel, that she could not hold her own among the giddy society of the Capitol, consequently, she had to retire."

Reader, imagine my thoughts when this "old thing" said she had to "retire," I did not know whether she had to be taken to a "dry dock" or be run into a "round house" for repairs, as I had never been used to a "Society" that was so giddy that innocent womanhood was forced to "retire," and I so stated to Mrs. Bigmouth, and she seemed very much surprised that I could not understand what "retire" from society meant.

She began by saying "that Miss Clara was visiting an Aunt in California," also stated that "her mother had gone back to Missouri and would not return to the Capitol." I explained my great sorrow at not getting to see Miss Clara before she left the city, as I felt it my duty to thank her for the courtesies and hospitality she had shown me, at which Mrs. Bigmouth heaved another sigh that resembled the buzz of a "June Bug" trying to escape from the tangled tresses of a red-headed woman.

She looked at me with a desperate glitter in her eyes, that seemed to say "you're a fool." However, I was as innocent as a lamb and could arrive at no conclusion why Miss Clara should "retire," and I again ventured to say that I hoped there would nothing serious come of her malady, at which Mrs. Bigmouth says, "Oh! Colonel, let's drop the subject, and had I known that you were so desperately in love with Clara Middlewest I never would have endeavored to make this explanation."

I assured the dear "old thing" that I was not in love with Clara, nor any other woman on earth, and further explained to her that I never was in Miss Clara's company in my life only just in a social way with others, as I had never met her only at public gatherings, therefore, I was at a loss to know how she could think for a moment that I was in love with her.

Mrs. Bigmouth squeezed out another sigh, and remarked, "Well, Colonel, that is the only thing that saved you." "Saved me?" says I. "What do you mean?"

"Has she been murdered, and do you think that had I ever been with her alone that I would have been accused of doing the poor girl bodily harm?"

She says. "No, no, Colonel no, I don't mean that." I was at that time in desperation, as I thought from what she had said that I must be connected, or almost connected with the affair, as she had said a few moments before that the only thing that saved me was by me never having been alone in her company.

Well, the old lady looked at me as though she thought I ought to be "bored for the simples," and remarked, "Well, Colonel, you must be the most innocent man in the whole world, or——" I said, "or what?" and she remarked in a whisper not intended for me to hear, "Blamed fool."

At this time our carriage was at the door of my hotel. I alighted and in a very gracious way thanked the dear "old thing" for her generosity in being so thoughtful of me, as I assured her that I had enjoyed the ride hugely and wound up my remarks by saying that I hoped at some time in the near future she would tell me all about Clara.

She slammed the carriage door to with a slam that as much as said "Oh! you idiot." However, I was just innocent enough not to know what this old scheming devil meant, nevertheless I afterwards learned that she actually thought I was in love with

Clara Middlewest, and she schemed up that ride to tell me all about Clara "retiring," in order that she might at once interest me and my Aunt's money in the welfare of her daughter, Dorothy.

In a day or two I was invited to Mrs. Bigmouth's residence again to a "blow out" in honor of her "dear daughter," and, of course, I went. About the first thing I said after getting there, was, well Mrs. Bigmouth, how is Clara, and when have you heard from her? I noticed that the old Lady's face looked like she had just come in off of a ten-mile run with the thermometer at a hundred and ten in the shade, and I also noticed that she gave me no reply, but gave me a look that made me feel like a "trade dollar."

In a few moments Mrs. Bigmouth came to me with a forty-cent smile, piled up all over her face, and said "Colonel, come into the library with me, I have some pictures I want to show you." I followed her, thinking that I was about to see a lot of rare old paintings.

The first picture she handed me was a photograph of old Mr. Middlewest, which was a very good likeness, indeed, and the next was a picture of the old lady, Mrs. Middlewest. Mrs. Bigmouth remarked after I had looked at both these pictures "that they had but one child, and her name was Clara," she at that time handed me Clara's photograph, which flattered her, indeed, as it was a fine likeness, and I did not hesitate to say so, in fact, I allowed myself to "rave" over Clara's beauty, however, about nine-tenths of it was "put on," as I had made up my mind to make Mrs. Bigmouth believe that I thought more of Clara than I actually did.

After I was through dilating upon the beauties of Clara, Mrs. Bigmouth handed me a picture of a sweet faced little girl baby, about four months old, and says "This is Clara's baby." (Whether it was or not, I am unable to say.) I gasped for breath and says: "I did not know that Clara was married." Mrs. Bigmouth says "SHE IS NOT, AND NEVER WAS."

All that I could think of was "retired."

Mrs. Bigmouth turned to me and says, "Now, Colonel Maple, I hope you understand what I have been trying to tell you for so long. Do you not?"

I simply said "Yes, ma'am." And I felt like a pair of yearling steers hitched to a four-horse load. I couldn't move.

Mrs. Bigmouth turned to me, and, in a haughty manner, asked, "Now, Colonel Maple, what do you think of Miss Clara, your dear Missouri friend?" And I remarked, as sarcastically as possible, "A Darn sight more than I do of those who associated with her and caused her downfall, and then because she was more unlucky, but just as good, turned their backs upon her and villified her, and at the same time were leading other innocent girls along the same slippery path that caused her to lose her character." 1, as politely as possible, asked Mrs. Bigmouth for my hat, and quietly left the house, as I was disgusted with such hypocrisy, and desired to show her my feelings regardless of what happened. Such is what "Fools" call "society," when, in reality, it is naught but the "Red light" that points the way to the brothel.

A MOTHER'S LAMENTATIONS— Oh! that my darling daughter had died before the blighting touch of "Fashionable Society" contaminated her pure soul

Chapter II.

The Downfall of Innocent Ruth Willmore, of Michigan, After Being Initiated Into Washington Society.

Hardly had the fate of Clara Middlewest passed into history, before another innocent country "ewe lamb" was led to the "slaughter pen" of Washington society.

Ruth Willmore was a country girl, who was blessed with everything that goes to make a loveable woman, as she possessed a sunny disposition, was fair of face and form, dreamy eyes and an intellect that was the pride of both her relatives and friends.

Willmore was not her real name, but Ruth was her given name, and we would not for the world call her by her real name, as her mother, two brothers and one sister still survive her, to mourn the fatal plunge that poor Ruth took into the maelstrom of society.

Ruth's father had died before she could hardly remember what a father's love and tender care meant, but she had a mother who possessed the sturdy qualities of a country lady. I mean by this, that she was industrious, frugal, possessing character, which is the bulwark and shield to humanity.

While Ruth's mother was forced to economize and even deprive herself of many things actually necessary and essential to make life happy, she did so without a murmur, as she knew by depriving herself of the necessities of life she would be better able to educate her children, and help to make them respected and honorable men and women.

Many who will read this book, will call to memory the fate of poor Ruth, as the State of Michigan, or, at least a large portion of her inhabitants, still remember the fate of this poor, miserable creature; however, this is the first time the true history of her awful fate was ever written. Not many knew the details, in fact only a score or two knew how ruthlessly this poor girl was enticed by the glitter and glamour of society, up, up, up to the dizzy heights of this seemingly white and innocent marble shaft of society, which rears itself aloft, and by its treacherous light beguiles the innocent girlhood of our fair land to mount to its heights, there to lose her virtue, honor, good name, in fact all that goes to make "woman" the emblem of innocence throughout the civilized world.

That marble shaft of society should be an emblem of virtue, honor and innocence, where girlhood could stand and feel assured that depraved manhood would be forced to halt at its base and given to understand that this is "Holy ground" and would be protected with every drop of the hearts blood of society.

But not so. Alas! It is to the contrary. While this "white shaft" looks innocent enough to the un-initiated, her pinnacle is crimsoned with virtue's blood, and her base is wet with the tears of indul-gent mothers, who were led astray by trusting the fickle light of society and placing her darling daugh-ter in the keeping of this gang of social pirates.

Ruth was a happy contented girl, just rounding into ripe womanhood, courted by a number of hon-orable country lads who loved her with a deep and tender love, which is an honor to any man, and a blessing to the woman who is so lucky as to be the object of such a love.

She had no desire to leave her country home, as her heart's treasures were there, consequently she had no longing to investigate the myths of "society's" fields. Ruth had read of fine city ladies, and gallant men, but her "Michigan home," dear mother, brothers and sister, with her country lovers was a "paradise" for her.

The fatal die had been cast, however, as her Uncle by marriage, had been elected to office from the great State of New York.

Of course the Willmore family were glad to know that "Uncle Theodore" had been chosen by his district to a seat in the lower House of Congress, but none of them ever dreamed that his election meant that poor Ruth was so soon to be given over to the yawning chasm of society's lust.

"Uncle Theodore" had married Ruth's mother's sister, and while they had been married nearly twenty years, no children had ever blessed the marriage, consequently Ruth's aunt was of course loath to have her husband go to the Capitol and leave her behind.

"Uncle Theodore" was a common miller who had run a grist mill all his life in a small rural town up in New York, and had been prosperous and content, loved by all who knew him, as he was noted for his

strict integrity, and always carried his pocket book
open to the wants of his neighbors and friends, and
no deserving man or woman ever went away empty
handed. He had been successful in a modest way
and had by his frugality and close attention to business accumulated considerable property, and had laid
by several thousand dollars in cash.

After he was elected to Congress, it is said the
old man was known to sit and weep bitter tears of
repentance that he had ever allowed his name to
be used in a POLITICAL way, as he actually re-
gretted his success at the polls on that drear November day.

But he was an honorable man, therefore in justice
to his friends who had championed his cause irre-
spective of politics, he felt it his bounden duty to
go to Washington and do the best he could for his
constituents.

His wife who was now about fifty years old, and
who had never been away from her husband any considerable length of time, could not bear the idea
of him going to Washington and leaving her behind;
therefore they concluded to dispose of their grist
mill and all other property they possessed, excepting
their little home, and both go to Washington for

the two years, resolved that at the end of "Uncle Theodore's" term that nothing on earth could induce him to "run for office again."

This point being settled and the property being disposed of, the next thing that perplexed "Aunt Amanda," as Amanda was her given name, was how she could manage to spend the long winter days alone in the great Capitol of the United States.

"Aunt Manda" was a woman who always "fretted" over something, and would magnify a small trouble into a national calamity, therefore each day when her husband would come to dinner, or return from his work at evening she would say, "Oh, I do not think I will go to Washington with you, as I can not bear to be left alone, and you will always be at the Capitol. No, I am not going."

This kept up until within a short while before her husband was to start for the Capitol, when the matter was settled by "Uncle Theodore" suggesting that they take Ruth Willmore with them as company for her.

This pleased "Aunt Amanda" hugely, and Ruth's mother was written in "post haste" and gave her consent, and Ruth was shipped at once to the little town up in New York to get ready to go to the Capitol.

Ruth, of course, poor child, was delighted, as it was an opportunity that seldom comes to any girl, much less a poor, obscure country girl. Ruth arrived at "Uncle Theodore's," and a more beautiful child of nature was never beheld.

After Ruth had retired for the night, "Uncle Theodore" says "Manda I have got the fever." "What fever" says "Aunt Amanda." "The Capitol fever, as with a little fixen Ruth will make us the most popular people in Washington, as she is the most beautiful child I ever looked at." He continued by saying "Manda here is one thousand dollars, and I want you to put every dressmaker in this town to work 'primping' you and that 'gal' up, as I have it in my head that Ruth Willmore will leave Washington the wife of some 'Nabob,' so don't spare money in 'fixing' that child to a 'Queen's taste."

"Aunt Amanda" felt in the same spirit, and the next morning every "Dressmaker" and "Milliner" in town was apprised of "Uncle Theodore's" plans and began to "fix" Ruth up to take Washington by storm.

"Uncle Theodore" had to suppliment his "thousand" several times before the day of leaving for the Capitol came, but he spent his money like a "Lord"

(4)

and Ruth was indeed the best dressed girl in that
section of New York State, and when Washington
laid eyes upon her, there was but little to criticise,
however "Uncle Theodore's" money soon corrected
the defects.

The day arrived to depart for Washington and
Ruth and "Aunt Amanda" were carted off to the
train with twelve or fourteen trunks packed jam full
of, not only good clothes, but fine ones in the pink
of fashion.

"Uncle Theodore" had gone to Washington some
two weeks before them and had rented a suite of
rooms at a fashionable resort, and awaited the coming of "Aunt Amanda" and Ruth with a marked
degree of impatience, as the old gentleman had im-
parted to many the fact that he had the prettiest
niece upon the face of the whole earth, and further
stated that she would get every cent he now had,
or ever would make, and he expected to make a few
million more before he died.

"Uncle Theodore" was a little "weak" upon the
subject of Ruth's beauty and was always talking
about it, consequently every one who had gotten
acquainted with him at his hotel was anxious to
see her.

The "old man" had learned that nothing "cut so much ice" at Washington as money, so while he did not tell any down right "falsehoods" about his wealth, his talk would lead any one to believe that two or three millions was only a small thing to him.

You know there is "no fool like an old fool" and it did really seem that "Uncle Theodore" had about gone "daffy" upon the subject of Ruth's beauty.

Well the day arrived for "Aunt Amanda" and Ruth to arrive, and "Uncle Theodore" had told several that morning, that he expected to "trot in" a girl that would cause the hearts of the male population of Washington to "thump the pudding out of their shirt fronts."

"Uncle Theodore" met them at the train, and, be it said to the credit of the old man's judgment that Ruth Willmore was a dream of beauty, in fact she would be noticed in particular, among ten thousand handsome women.

"Uncle Theodore" engaged a "swell turn out" and brought "Aunt Amanda" and Ruth to the hotel, and pretty soon their trunks followed, and the great number was evidence of their wealth.

The two had their lunch served in their rooms, as both the ladies were tired, but "Uncle" told them they must "rig up" for "dinner."

"Aunt Amanda" and Ruth wanted to know what he meant by saying "dinner" as it was now about "supper time." The old man says, H-u-s-h—the aristocrats have cut the word supper clean out of the dictionary, and from now on we only have "breakfast," "lunch," and "dinner."

Well, Ruth "fixed up" in the swellest rig she had, and "Aunt Amanda" followed suit, and "Uncle Theodore" arrayed himself in a "swallow tailed" coat, that made him look like a "thoroughbred" and about nine o'clock they marched down to "dinner." The dining room was jammed with "Society" and many of them were eager to behold that "Michigan beauty" that the "Old Man" from New York had been talking about, as "Uncle Theodore" had been "dubbed" the "Old Man from New York."

The male members of society especially were anxious to behold Miss Ruth, and the ladies were anxious to "hate her" if she really was beautiful.

The happy moment of the "Old Man's" life had arrived, as he marched down the long aisle of the Dining Room with "Aunt Amanda" on one arm and Ruth upon the other. The "Flunky" parted the drapery and a flood of light fell square upon the trio, as they marched into the Dining Room.

When they first entered a babble of voices could be heard, as both male and female were endeavoring to talk at the same time, however their "talk" is always "chaffy" the same as their brains, as society has fewer brains to the square inch than any class of "things" that ever infested the earth.

But "Uncle Theodore" and his "Michigan Beauty" surely silenced their "jabber" as every eye of both "he," "she" and "it" was fixed upon this trio, and of course Ruth was the attraction.

Reader, I was present in that Dining Room, and I never beheld a more beautiful creature, and my judgment was the same as every man who beheld Ruth Willmore, as she came down the aisle that December night, as innocent as a new born babe.

The "Old Man" had dilated to me upon Ruth's beauty, and many, many times I felt it my duty to warn him, and advise him, in the name of God to leave her in Michigan, but I lacked the manhood and moral courage to do it, and thousands of times since I have reproached myself for not warning him, as I might have been able to save her from what befell her.

I did not meet Ruth that night, however, to my certain knowledge she was introduced to twenty-three

human hyenas, who parade as "men." She was also
smothered by the female contingent of this society
"gang," and, oh reader, did it ever appear to you
that the female degenerates of this society tribe is
to be more dreaded than the male members, as they
play the part of "friend" to innocent girlhood in
order to be able to more surely lead them to their
awful fate, as they consider the sooner they are
"retired" the better it is for them, as a society woman
hates with the hatred of hell, an innocent and beautiful woman, as she has long since learned that a
"true man" admires "true womanhood."

I left the Dining Room in disgust, as my conscience was lashing me for not having the manhood
to have warned this old Uncle what would befall his
Niece, did he not watch her day and night, but alas,
alas, I procrastinated, and this girl who came to
Washington as innocent and as pure as the rose
which clambered up the walls of her humble Michigan home, was sacrificed to appease the depraved
desire of what we call "Elegant society,' while in
fact it is only a band of devils, both male and female,
seeking whom they may devour.

On opening my mail the following morning I
received an invitation from Mrs. Gayfrock, a widow

of a United States Senator. who lived on Pennsylvania Avenue, requesting my presence at her home upon the next evening to take lunch.

I accepted, and the thought struck me that I would ease my conscience, and at the same time be a protector to Ruth in taking her to this social function, as Mrs. Gayfrock had given the gentlemen the privilege to bring a lady friend.

I at once wrote a short note to her Uncle, as I had not "met" Miss Ruth, and explained to him my desire, as I was quite sure that her Uncle had been favorably impressed with me, but in a few moments I was handed a note which read:

"Dear Colonel:—I appreciate your modest manner in letting your invitation to Mrs. Gayfrock's party to my Niece come through me, but I am pained to inform you that my Niece will attend this party with Senator A's son, Alonzo.

"Yours truly,
"THEODORE R——."

I received the note and felt as though my veins would burst trying to control my anger, as Alonzo A. was one of the most disreputable mortals that ever went unhung, however he had money at his command, which was all that "rotten society" demands.

The evening of Mrs. Gayfrock's party arrived and I went without a lady friend, as I had fully made up my mind that the evening should be spent in keeping my eye upon Alonzo A. and this innocent Michigan girl.

As usual the same aristocrats (?) were at the party and after the regular nonsensical ceremonies of the early evening was over, supper was announced and wine and champagne followed in close touch.

I had no lady with me, therefore I was accorded the "honor seat" the head of the table, consequently I was first served. I had made up my mind that I was going to warn Ruth of her danger at all hazards so when Mrs. Gayfrock glided up to me with her "cut glass bottle" of wine to serve me, I deliberately turned my glass up side down and said. "Never so long as I live will I ever again taste wine or champagne, especially in the presence of ladies, as no gentleman can afford to set an example for another man's sister, which he would not allow his own sister to follow, and no true gentleman can think as much of a lady after she drinks wine as he can before, and no true gentleman will allow a lady to do it if he can prevent it."

Away down about the middle of the table, a little

golden haired girl hysterically clapped her dainty hands, and this little angel was Ruth Willmore, while the remainder of these "she devils" gave me a look that would have a tendency to "freeze your feet." Mrs. Gayfrock says, "Oh, Colonel, when did you join the Salvation Army?" Of course this gang of degenerates had a laugh at my expense, however, I stoutly lived up to my statement and refused to taste society's "strychnine."

Not another one refused to drink wine around the table until Mrs. Gayfrock reached Ruth, when she said "Please Mamm, I do not care for wine." When Alonzo, the arch schemer from the paradise of devils dared to make fun of her as being "one of Colonel Maple's Salvation Army recruits." Ruth was young and inexperienced, and soon yielded to Alonzo's entreaties, and I sat by and saw this virtuous Michigan lass take her first plunge into the abyss of shame.

Not only one drink but several did Ruth take, that night, and after the second drink her cheeks became flushed from the awful effects of that awful drug, and within an hour from that time I actually beheld that girl, who a few hours before was as innocent as "The lily of the valley" unblushingly place her foot upon the knee of her escort to have him tie her dainty slipper.

Before the evening was over she had drank more wine, and was "mixing" with this strange crowd of "society degenerates" with as much ease as though she was a veteran, and had been brought up in the midst of such debauchery. In order to urge her on and make sure of her downfall, whenever she would display her utter abandonment, the crowd, both men and women would applaud her, which of course led her to believe in her bewildered condition, that she was making the hit of her life.

Alonzo the "Ape" she was with, had the audacity to come up to me and remark. "Colonel, your convert, Miss Willmore, is a sample of all such d—— foolish twaddle about temperance."

I simply remarked "that my sentiments were those of a gentleman, therefore I did not know whether he could comprehend their meaning."

He says in return, "Old man there will be a tomorrow, and a day of settlement for these insults."

I was disguested and ready to leave, but I was determined to stay until the "debauch" was over in order to protect Ruth if possible.

About four o'clock every one but myself and Mrs. Gayfrock was as full as "ticks," poor Ruth not being used to this sort of thing, it had made her deathly sick, and I suggested to Mrs. Gayfrock that she be taken home. "NEVER, in this condition, asserted Alonzo." "Why?" I remarked. "If it is no harm to drink the vile stuff, why should you care for her Uncle and Aunt to see her drunk?" and I emphasized the word "Drunk,' for says I, "Like begets like," and just as sure as you drink it, just that sure you will get "Drunk."

"Colonel Maple, I want you to understand that I am the escort of Miss Willmore," says Alonzo, "and I will see that she is taken care of. I will call my carriage and drive her around a few blocks in the crisp air, and she will be all right." I simply remarked, "No you don't drive Miss Willmore around for a few blocks nor for a few minutes, unless I am with you, as I know your motive." He at once flew into a frenzy and fired his revolver at me, the ball lodging in the fleshy part of my thigh, which I carry to this day as a "Memento" of one of Washington's grand "Social" (?) functions.

Ruth was driven home by Mrs. Gayfrock in a maudlin condition, and it was explained to her Uncle and Aunt that the ball room was so hot she fainted and these poor old simple minded country folks believed it.

The next morning there was a column and a half in the leading daily papers of Washington, about the grand social, and brilliant gathering at the residence of Mrs. Gayfrock, the charming widow of the deceased Senator—but bear in mind not a word said about this grand (?) social (?) function breaking up in a row and Colonel Dick Maple getting shot in the leg.

The funny part of the matter is, that these same papers had a large headline stating that "Col. Dick Maple" while carelessly toying with his "target pistol" had accidentally discharged it, inflicting a slight flesh wound in his thigh, however the wound was only slight, and he would soon be out again."

Now, reader, you may think this strange, but I actually was "whipped" into giving this newspaper tale the color of truth, as I tried in every conceivable manner to secure the arrest of Alonzo, but I could not, as he had money, therefore he was proof against arrest in the glorious City of Washington, the Capitol of the United States, and after I could not secure his arrest, I actually told my friends I accidentally shot myself.

After I could not get a warrant for Alonzo, I concluded to do the next best thing, so I made up my mind to go to Ruth's Uncle and Aunt, and tell them what had happened, and warn them what to expect if they did not keep a keen look out, as Ruth was young, and Washington society was rotten to the core.

I called at the "Old Man's" Hotel, and sent up my card, and instead of being invited up to the old gentleman's parlor, he came down to the "Lobby" of the Hotel, and when he reached me I could see he was very much excited and I asked him if anything serious had happened. "Serious," he snorted, "I think it is a serious matter for a gentleman of your standing to attend a social gathering of well bred people as you did at Mrs. Gayfrock's, and get beastly "drunk" and break up the party in a regular wild west fashion." I was perfectly astounded, and began by saying, "My Dear Sir," however the old gentleman would not allow me to finish the sentence, and flatly told me that the Senator's son Alonzo, also Mrs. Gayfrock had informed him of my conduct, and further stated that it was my boisterous conduct that had caused his Niece to faint. He told me that I was mad because I did not get to take Miss Ruth to the party, and had gone there deliberately to disgrace myself and all that was there, and he did not want me to come whining around him, and further stated if I did he would use a "Horse-whip" on me.

I saw it was useless to try to argue the case with him, therefore turned my back on him, and the last thing I heard him say was "You rich blackguard."

Reader this is the outcome of Washington society, and this is the treatment I received in en-deavoring to snatch dear, sweet Ruth Willmore from the very jaws of a life of shame.

I remained in Washington for several months afterwards, and watched the course of this country girl, and exactly five months from the day she arrived in that great city of "shams and sharks" poor Ruth, one bright morning in May ended her career by cut-ting her poor throat from ear to ear with an ivory handled knife which belonged to a manacuring set this fiend "Alonzo" had given her. Why did she do it? Oh! Reader, ask that old heart broken mother, who still lives in Michigan ask those brothers and that sister. Ask that dear old Aunt and Uncle who still live in the great State of New York, and their answer will be Beware! Beware! "Uncle Theodore" and "Aunt Amanda" still remember me, and many are the letters I have received from those dear old souls, begging me to pardon them for their harsh judgment, as they have long since learned that my motives were based upon the eternal laws of justice and that my actions were prompted in behalf of virtue, but my warning was not heeded, and virtue paid the penalty.

In the State of Michigan today you will find in a country graveyard a marble slab, with no other inscription upon it but "Ruth." No mention of her life, no word of consolation for her friends, but simply "Ruth."

Oh! Mothers and Fathers, travel across the continent with your daughters to that cold slab of marble, and while there read this chapter, with uncovered heads, and point to that silent monument of man's perfidy, and woman's confidence, and pray God that no such fate may overtake the darlings of your bosoms.

"THE WAGES OF SIN IS DEATH." — Beautiful Grace Frankness of Pennsylvania hangs herself to hide her shame, after being wrecked by Washington Society.

Chapter III.

The Awful Story of a Trusting and Loving Mother.

I have been writing of what I saw in "Washington Society" but now intend to relate the experiences of the wife of a gentleman who served four terms in the lower House of Congress from the State of Pennsylvania, and who retired a poorer but wiser man, but being a man of strict integrity and honorable motives, left the Capitol without a single taint upon his individual character, and who is loved by his friends for his moral courage.

There will not be a dozen well posted persons in the State of Pennsylvania who will read this chapter, but could call the name of the lady whose experience in "Washington Society" I will now relate

[67]

as she is identified, not only in her own state with
temperance work, but has a national reputation for
her noble service in rescuing "fallen women" all
over the United States, and who has a host of warm
friends in every State in the Union.

We will know her as Mrs. Hattie M. Frankness,
"Hattie M." is a part of her real name.

Mrs. Frankness had heard of my endeavors to
write a book of this kind and felt it her duty to
"cast in her mite," therefore, addressed to me the
following letter:

"Dear Mr. Maple:

"You may think it strange to receive this letter
from me as I have never been permitted to meet
you, but I have learned through a mutual friend that
you were writing a book founded upon the awful
condition of society among the rich, and those who
presume to set the example for the masses. Myself
and husband have often talked the matter over along
the same lines as I understand you are writing upon,
and since our sad experience in Washington with our
darling children while my husband was endeavoring to do his duty as an official.

"I would like to add my sad chapter to your great
book. However, it is a bitter undertaking, for it is
a chapter wet with the tears of a mother's grief, but I
deem it my duty as a wife and mother.

"I beg to ask if you could grant me a small space in your book for the recital of my awful experience, as I deem it my duty to God and the innocent girls of our beloved land, and as a warning to mothers.

"Hoping to hear from you at once, relative to this matter, and bidding you God's speed in your laudible undertaking, I am,

"Sincerely yours,

(MRS.) HATTIE M. FRANKNESS."

As soon as I received Mrs. Frankness' letter, knowing her by reputation, I did not wait to write her but at once arranged to go to her home and get in detail her experience, well knowing that she had an awful tale to relate, else she would not have written me this letter, therefore I proceeded to her home which is an unostentatious, but a cozy seven-room house, situated near the historic "Anthracite Coal Fields."

Oh! what a pleasure to meet such a lady. A lady highly educated and who had been given every advantage in childhood, and who had been raised in the lap of plenty, but who possessed that lovable womanly spirit that throws off the sweet aroma of purity.

I tramped up to her door with "grip" in hand, and

found this lady "stringing beans" for dinner, upon
the back porch of her farm cottage, and humming
that good old soul stirring hymn, "Rocked in the
Cradle of the Deep."

I gently knocked at the open door, as I felt it was
a sin to disturb that beautiful scene, as it would
have been a grand sitting for the brush of an old
master.

Mrs. Frankness arose, brushed the "bean hulls"
from her apron, and came forward to greet me, and
Oh, what a greeting. She simply said "Come in,"
but it sounded in my ears, just like I imagine the
voice of Jesus would sound when he says "Come
home" to a weary soul, as she did not ask what I
wanted or who I was, but simply with a motherly
smile said "Come in."

I had forgotten what I wanted and who I was,
as I had never received such a welcome, save from
that silvery haired mother in old Indiana.

She overwhelmed me with her simple reception,
and for the time being, I had forgotten everything
but the consciousness of knowing that I was near
the habitation of Angels.

At last I gathered my "wits" and handed her my
card which read simply "Dick Maple." She looked

at me for a moment, with tears glistening in her eyes, then gently clasped my hand and said, "I am so glad to see you that I need help to enjoy my happiness," and at once stepped to the edge of the back porch and gave a rope which was connected to an old fashioned dinner bell a few pulls, and each clang of that old dinner bell was sweeter to me than the grandest music I had ever heard, as it reminded me of my boyhood days before my "Aunt's" money had weaned me from nature. Presently a broad shouldered, sunburned man of perhaps sixty years of age, came in sight and halted at the old well in the yard and drank deep from that "Old Moss Covered Bucket" and proceeded towards the back door.

He entered and Mrs. Frankness with an ease that plainly marked her a cultured lady said "Husband this is Colonel Maple from Indiana."

Mr. Frankness with the ease and unassuming dignity of a thorough gentleman, as he was, simply said "Colonel, nowhere could you be more welcome."

I will now give the reader an introduction to Mr. Frankness, and then proceed to take up the experience of Mrs. Frankness in society, and will omit the details of my very happy visit to the home of this

very elegant family however, the reader must know
in a slight degree something about Mr. Frankness.

He was a man about six feet, two inches tall,
broad shouldered, and his hair was once very black,
but at this time would be called "Iron gray."

He was a man of culture, having a polished education, and it is said was one of the most powerful
orators to be found anywhere in the Eastern States,
which is saying a great deal, as "The East" has had
the honor of producing many powerful orators.

He was simplicity personified, and made no at-
tempt whatever to impress you with his learning,
but on the contrary would rather listen than talk.

He had quit politics because, as he said, "he
desired to be a gentleman, without having to fight
to keep from becoming a rascal."

He was a devout Christian, as well as his wife,
and believed in God "in all things."   ,

This, dear reader, I think will give you an idea
of Mr. Frankness.

As stated before, I will not relate all of the many
pleasant circumstances connected with my stay at
the home of this most elegant lady and gentleman,
but will proceed to relate word for word, as near as
possible Mrs. Frankness' experience with the abomin-

ations of society, and I herewith reproduce it in her exact language. Her story follows:

"I was born and brought up to womanhood in the State of North Carolina, my Father and Mother moving to Pennsylvania when I was seventeen years old.

"I married Mr. Frankness at the age of nineteen. We have been married about thirty-eight years. My Father was a farmer of some means and Mr. Frankness was also a farmer when I married him. I was educated in a Female Seminary in Nashville, Tenn.

"Several years after we were married, Mr. Frankness was induced to run for Congress. He consented to do so, being elected for four consecutive terms. However, after the first two terms he always received the nomination without asking for it, and against his wishes, as he had learned that the professional politician was a thing to be abhored, consequently desired to get out of politics, also knowing that I was not in sympathy with all of his political views, I being a Southerner and naturally having some ideas in sympathy with the Southern people, and Mr. Frankness being a staunch Republican, of course, at times we did not see political things exactly alike. This was not the greatest reason however, why we did not want to remain in politics, as we had two daughters and one son who was in a manner grown, and we did not want to risk blasting their lives by allowing them to come in contact with society's filthy crater, as we had silently watched both young men and women approach that volcano of 'seething shame' called 'society' and for a moment hesitate, but eventually plunge in to emerge lost to honor, lost to the entreaties of friends, lost to reason, and evetually lost to God.

"I, and the children had spent each winter with Mr. Frankness in Washington, during his first four years, always retiring to our farm in the summer. Our children were growing up, in fact our son and Grace, our oldest daughter were then about of age, and we concluded after my husband was elected for the third term to rent our farm and move to Washington. Oh! If I could only undo this one act of my life, I would be willing to live in a hovel the remainder of my days, and exist upon bread and water."

Right here Mrs. Frankness broke down and wept bitter tears of repentance, and she remarked "Oh! Colonel Maple, I can not see how I can proceed with these awful facts, as they tear open anew the terrible lacerations of my poor heart, placed there by that demon-faced, and hideous harlot called 'fashionable society,' and was it not for the good of the rising generation, I could never relate this horrible story that involves my own flesh and blood, and my darling daughter Grace, and my fickle son Harold."

"I was moved to tears by this noble woman's distress, and suggested that she keep her secret locked in her poor broken heart, but she replied, "They are gone, and this story of society's crime, can do them no harm and it may be the means of snatching some halting mother's darling from the pit of society's abomination, and sure disgrace."

Mrs. Frankness was so wrought up and broken hearted that the task was postponed until the following day.

That evening just about sundown I was strolling through the orchard, and my attention was attracted by a voice in solemn supplication, imploring a living God for courage to perform her duty. I listened and soon learned that the voice emanated from the lips of that dear old Mother whose heart had been gashed by society's poisoned and unmerciful dagger. Oh! what a prayer. I uncovered my head as I felt that I was standing upon holy ground. I never moved while that tormented soul beseeched power from the Great White Throne to perform her duty.

Ah! could the heartless rabble of society have heard that mother's supplication, methinks that the jingle of wine glasses would have ceased; the cheek flushed with wine would have paled; the giddy clatter of tongues would have hushed; and the seducers of virtue would have called upon their God for mercy, as that prayer was burdened with mercy for those who had wrought the destruction of her darling children, and brought sorrow and disgrace upon their parents.

I returned to the house in a round-about way, as I did not want this distressed soul to know that I had heard her supplication as I felt my unworthiness to even listen to such a righteous plea from one so near the Throne.

When I returned to the House, Mrs. Frankness and her husband were sitting upon the front porch, gently singing "Nearer My God to Thee," and a more happy contented couple it has never been my lot to behold. The face of Mrs. Frankness was as placid as that of a sleeping babe, and the thought struck me "I know that my Redeemer lives" as God's approval was so plainly stamped upon that heartbroken Mother's face, that any one would know that she had not gone to her Lord in vain

As I took a seat with them, Mrs. Frankness remarked "Colonel Maple, we will proceed tomorrow with our task and we will have no more interruptions."

Well I knew that she had obtained from "The mercy seat" the full assurance that she was right.

The morning came, and Mrs. Frankness began her sorrowful story by saying "We moved to Washington, where the purest of men and women should reside, but Oh it is the exception and not the rule, that you find integrity and honor at the Capitol of the greatest nation on earth.

"I, like thousands of other foolish mothers thought that my children could not be induced to go astray, as they had never had aught but good examples set before them, therefore foolishly believed that my children could not be led astray by the false lights of deceptive society, however I was not acquainted with the awful cunning of what society is pleased to call the 'Smart set' or the 'Four hundred.'

"We had always been frugal and had saved some money each year since we had been married, and in the four years of my husband's official career we had saved each year more than half of his salary, conse-

. quently we had several thousand dollars saved by the
time we made the 'fatal move.'

   "We rented a modest home in a respectable part
of the city of Washington, surrounded by the families of Senators, Congressmen and other officials,
and within a very short time, and before we actually
realized it, we had drifted into the treacherous current of Society which surely leads to the 'Niagara'
of shame and dishonor.

"Once in this current, it is not an easy matter
to turn back, nor even check your frail craft, especially when you have allowed your children to taste
of such pleasures, as you can not reason with them
as you could with more mature minds. Again you
can not always be with your children, therefore you
are compelled to 'trust to fate' very often, and you
know that 'fate' may mean most anything, however, in our case it meant the blacking of the character of both poor Grace and Harold, my darling
children.

"The first time that I detected the filthy touch of
society's grime upon my dear son, was upon his
return from a 'social,' given by one of our neighbors
who played the part of a Christian lady. Oh! Colonel I detest 'socials,' I mean where you have to be-

come 'drunk' to be social. Yes, the first time I noticed the cankerous touch of society upon Harold was upon his return from this 'social' given by this seeming pious old lady, whom I afterwards learned, not only to be a rank hypocrite, but was actually addicted to the drink habit. Harold returned home and I noticed his cheeks were flushed, and his talk was unnatural, and I detected the smell of this devilish drug upon his breath.

"I questioned him and he confessed that he had drank a quantity of wine at the home of my supposed Christian friend.

"Oh! I plead with that dear boy upon bended knees to promise me that he never would again touch the abominable stuff and he made the promise and I believe in good faith, but Oh! how hard to keep a good resolve when this profligate gang of vagabonds, who parade as the 'chosen few' make fun and tantalize one for a laudable resolution.

"Not long until Harold returned home again under the influence of liquor. Once more with tears streaming down my face I exacted a promise and once more he gave the promise, and renewed the resolve, only to be broken again.

"I resolved to move back to the farm in Pennsylvania, and announced our intentions, when to our great astonishment Harold informed me that we could go if we liked, but as far as he was concerned he intended to stay in Washington.

"Mother like, I clung to the word 'Hope' and thought it better to stay in Washington and try to reclaim him, than to leave him, and let him go to destruction without an effort to save him.

"Ah! better had we allowed this boy to go to destruction than to have sacrificed dear Grace, who was then as pure as the brook that ripples down the slope of yonder mountain, but God will forgive a poor mother's mistakes, as I did what I thought best, and stayed in Washington, and not only fed to the monster, 'society' my boy, but stood by and saw Grace my darling daughter sacrificed to that gang of unGodly beasts, who would have you believe they were 'men' and 'women,' when they are a disgrace to the land that gave them birth.

"Harold went from bad to worse, until—Oh, Colonel Maple, must I tell you? Yes, I have promised God that I would give this to the world for the benefit of the living—until he was killed in a 'brothel, mingling with the self same gang that once paraded in society as the 'elite of society.'

"Harold was killed by over confidence in his early training, but I have learned to my sorrow that early training can not withstand the onslaught of the devil who is backed by society, as the devil has learned that he can make the young believe that what society sanctions, must be all right, therefore he attacks the young with society marshalled at his back, and the citadel of their early training is soon stormed, and the sharp hoofs of society's demons have absolute control, while mothers and fathers warnings are treated as 'foggy' ideas, until too late the victim has crossed the 'dead line' where mothers' prayers and mothers' tears, are lost upon the desert of blasted hopes and blasted ambitions.

"After Harold had met his awful fate at the hands of society, we then fully made up our minds to return to our Pennsylvania home, but in the meantime Mr. Frankness had been elected the fourth and last time to another term in Congress. Oh, I hate the name of 'Politician' as I know them so well, and I know their actions, and the unholy tribe they cater to.

"No matter if my husband had been elected to another term, I was resolved to return to our country home, where I could protect the remainder of

(6)

my brood from the scheming 'hawks' and 'buzzards' of society.

"I and my husband had had many talks about Grace and her future, as we had noticed of late that Grace had been coming home rather late from social gatherings, but Oh God, I dared not dream of a wrong intention, as I was still blind to the awful snares of society, and blind still in the confidence of the early training of my children, especially my darling girls; however, Alice was only fourteen years old, and was always at home with myself and her father.

"I hesitated to make any inquiries of Grace why she staid out so late to these parties, as I did not want her to think I believed it possible for her to do a wrong, or an unlady like act, as I never believed in letting your children know that you believed them anything but honorable.

"However, Grace's hours became so uncertain that I was compelled to make an investigation, and Oh, imagine my horror, on learning that she too one night was led to my door by a policeman, under the influence of this damnable drug 'Rum.' I prayed God to take me, so that I might never have to behold the like again.

"I prayed with Grace and a more penitent child

I never beheld, and she told me that she had only drank 'just one glass' and I poor ignorant soul believed it. She stated that Mrs. 'F.' had insisted that I take just one glass as it would do me no harm, and I did, and the effect was almost instantaneous, and Mrs. F had come to within half a block of home with me and then had asked a policeman to see me home.'

"I forgave her, but made up my mind that we would at once leave Washington. Within a day or two I informed Grace that we would move back to Pennsylvania on the next Thursday, when to my surprise Grace flatly refused to go, stating that I could take her back, but the first opportunity she had she would 'run off' as she did not propose to live in the country.

"I was not going to run any further risk, so regardless of Grace's threats we moved back to the farm, and Grace at once became changed, her sweet disposition was transformed into a morose fault finding one, however I tried to make home as happy as possible, in fact I invited her girl friends to see us from Washington, and endeavored to keep the house full of company, thinking that perhaps I could change her longing for fickle and unholy society, but alas, alas, how utterly I falied.

"On a Tuesday morning the 17th day of December after we had returned to our country home, Alice was sent up to Grace's room about six o'clock in the morning to awaken her, as it was her custom to do, and I will never forget the scream this poor child uttered, as she had pushed the door of Grace's room open and beheld her poor sister's dead body hanging from the transom. Her face black from strangulation, as she had stole out during the night, secured a rope and hanged herself from the transom of her own room.

"Oh Colonel Maple, I am about to repeat something to you that I have never told or repeated to any one on earth, not even to Grace's dear father, as I had concluded to bear the shame alone, and did not want to burden Mr. Frankness with the terrible shame; however a few evenings since I fell upon my knees alone in our orchard and prayed as I had never prayed before for 'light' how to proceed in giving you facts for your noble book, and it was plainly revealed to me that I should hold back nothing, as it was revealed to me by God that his blessings should be upon me for so doing, therefore Colonel Maple, you are the first mortal that I ever have repeated what I am about to repeat.

"We let the neighbors believe that Grace hung herself on the account of being deprived of her Washington associates, and from a girlish belief that she was being imposed upon, but Oh, God, this, this is the true story Colonel Maple," at the same time handing me a yellow crumpled piece of paper, scribbled in a school girl's hand.

"Dear Mamma, Papa and Alice: A few months would reveal my secret, therefore I deem it best to cover my shame as much as possible in the cold embrace of death, as no one need ever know the reason for my rash act.

"Forgive me Mamma, Papa and little Alice, as God has already forgiven me.   GRACE."

"This Colonel Maple," continued the distracted Mother, "is why I wrote you the letter I did, and caused you to come from Indiana to listen to a heart-broken mother's story.

"I, a poor heart-broken Mother have been forced to furnish two precious lives to appease the hellish lust of society.

"Alice, poor child, died in a few weeks after Grace's self destruction, but thank God I know she died an honorable death."

With a look now of utter dispair Mrs. Frankness

exclaimed. "Now, Colonel Maple, you have my secret, Tell it to the world. Tell it to Mothers. Tell it to the fair girlhood of the land. Proclaim it to the young men of the nation. Tell the word that 'society' has robbed me of not only my own blood and flesh, but stole the good name of my forefathers as far as possible. Let this story of 'Society's Crime' be read from the frozen North to the balmy Southland, my native home."

ONCE HANDSOME MRS. FLORENCE MATTINGLY:— This miserable creature was once considered the most handsome woman in Wisconsin, but "Fashionable" Chicago society wrecked not only herself, but her two beautiful daughters and a loving husband

Chapter IV.

The Story of a Once Happy Wife, Who Was Ruined by "Society's Contaminating Breath.

Could we but gather together from the four corners of the earth, the wrecks of Society's Tornado, we could march through this land with an army of blasted lives that would so appall this generation that society's touch would be shunned and dreaded as that of the leper!

"Society" is not satisfied to blast the lives of the young, but she halts her "Chariot of Sin" before the door of the happy home, and marches across the threshold of that home, with the smile and face of an angel, but under her deceitful tongue is found the posion of the asp, and the hideous remorse of a lost soul in hell.

[89]

Society does not come to her victim with an open book, recorded therein the miseries and shame of girls who were once the pride of a loving mother's and father's heart.

She does not unfurl her black flag of harlotism; she does not hang her chart of dark deeds upon the wall of your happy home and point out thereon the crimson spots left by her unholy touch; but she comes arrayed as an angel, and whispers into your willing ear that there are greater things which you should behold, and which she will show you for the asking.

Remember this "Chariot of Sin" does not halt at your door unless there are one of three attractions to be found.

First: If you have a beautiful daughter, fair of face and form and one who some male member of that despicable herd of "human hyenas" desire to debauch, then this "Chariot of Sin" will halt at your door and pass in her perfumed card to the mother of that girl, as society well knows that the easiest way to accomplish her most diabolical end is to flatter and cajole a loving mother by making her believe that her daughter is one of the most beautiful girls on earth, and with the proper management, and properly placing her before the aristocratic world that she will outshine and out-rival any in that most elegant (?) set.

That poor mother believing that this bundle of perfidy of her own sex could not be competent of scheming for the destruction of her darling daughter, relies implicitly upon this bundle of shams.

Second: If you are wealthy and have a son who some female member of society desires to entice into her meshes to enable her to "bleed" this fickle lad of his wealth, in order that she may dress in "purple and fine linen," she will cross your threshold and it is very seldom that society fails in her mission, especially when she reaches out her bejeweled hand and promises social victory, but alas, alas, she never intimates to that mother or father what her real mission is, for did she knock at your door and plainly tell you her exact mission, you would treat her as though she was from the pest house, with a thousand contagious diseases clinging to her silken garments.

Third: Her most unholy mission is when she halts her splendidly appointed "Chariot of Shame" in front of that happy home where the husband is

all love, and where that beautiful wife sits in contentment and bliss, day in and day out, dreaming day
dreams of her husband, whom she considers the one
great man among the men of the earth and gazes upon
her children as they prattle in innocent play, and
considers them as a bevy of angels sent direct from
God to multiply her blessings.

We watch that loving wife as she stands upon
that vine clad porch of her happy home and shades
her eyes and gazes down the road, anxious and
eager to catch a glimpse of her husband, returning
from some business mission; we watch him approach-
ing that dear wife of his bosom; his breast heaving
with manly pride, and see that dear wife who is the
picture of contentment throw her arms about him in
an ecstasy of joy and behold that happy man implant
upon the brow of that most happy wife the pure kiss
of a pure man.

We see them at eventide resting in the quiet
gloaming with their children playing in childish glee
about their feet, and we exclaim "Oh! this must be
the zenith of happiness."

Society must be depraved indeed, when she drags
her filthy form across the threshold of a mother's
confidence and robs her of her son or daughter, but

Oh! what a hideous creature she must be when she unblushingly knocks at the door of the happy home of husband and wife and there stealthily drops the seed of discontent into the heart of that wife, and holds the torch of deception in her bejeweled hand.

The reader may think that such an act could only be performed by a demon of hell, who had been there for centuries, being tutored to perform such a fiendish mission, but Oh! not so, as this "harlot" of society has been for decades past, tramping up and down through the length and breadth of this land, parading herself as the "Anointed of the land," halting thither and yon at the door of contented homes and dragging to their eternal fate, girls who were satisfied with their lot until she planted the seed of discontent within their simple hearts and whispered promises rose tinted with the grandeur of fame and social prestige, but never daring to tell them that a short distance after this rose tinted journey had begun that the springs of desolation would bubble forth from every hillock, and the rivers of despair in hellish darkness flowed on forever, her bosom covered with blackened characters of the young from every walk of life, and at her destination were piled mountain high, the dead hopes and ambitions;

the ruined characters and good names of her innumerable host of dupes who had succumbed to her rose tinted promises that were never fulfilled, and from that festering putrifying heap of lost characters the stench has become so oppressive that the world has begun to look upon this "demon eyed" harlot as a thing to be dreaded and despised above all others.

We make the above statement in order to better prepare the reader for what is to follow, as the remainder of this chapter will be taken up with the recital of the story of a once happy and contented wife, and mother, but who was led astray by the cunning and deceitful tongue of society.

The recital of this woman's woes are verbatim, as she wrote it herself, and we give it to the world, believing that it will so impress itself upon the minds of the reader that they will be fully prepared to detect this awful "Harlot" should she ever present herself with her fine equipage at the door of your home.

This woman was once the loved and contented wife of a manufacturer of the City of Chicago, who was not rich, as some would deem riches, but who, perhaps, was worth fifty or sixty thousand dollars, and whose income was ten or twelve thousand dollars a year,, therefore you can see, he was considered by all, to be a very prosperous man.

He had been raised in the country up in the State of Wisconsin, his father being a blacksmith, but who had by his thrift been able to give his children a fair education, and his son Wilbur had the genius of his father and could fashion iron to suit his will, therefore had patented a very useful invention which is used today by tens of thousands of housewives in connection with their cook stoves.

The public soon recognized the value of this small invention and the demand became so great that Wilbur Mattingly moved to Chicago in order to be better prepared to manufacture his invention.

Wilbur was his first name, and Mattingly, sounds a good deal like his surname, but it is not.

Before leaving his Wisconsin home for the great western metropolis he proposed to, and was accepted by the very beautiful daughter of Rev. Andrew W., and they were married by Rev. Mr. W., he being a Methodist "Circuit Rider."

Florence W. was a graceful, and very beautiful girl, in fact the "folks" in that little Wisconsin town declared upon her wedding day that Wilbur

Mattingly had married the most beautiful girl in all Wisconsin.

As soon as the "Infair" was over, Wilbur and his beautiful country bride left for Chicago, their future home.

They at first rented a four room cottage on the outskirts of the city, as they had but a small amount of capital and desired to put as much money in the manufacturing plant as possible.

But a happier and more contented pair never occupied a four room cottage in Chicago or any other City.

Wilbur's business began growing from the first week he opened up, as he had already created a considerable demand for his invention, therefore no young married couple ever star.ed in life with brighter prospects.

Within two years Wilbur had to move to larger quarters, as the demand for his invention had so increased that he could not fill the orders, therefore a three-story building was rented and the large sign across the top of the building read "THE MAT-TINGLY MANUFACTURING CO."

As Wilbur had within two years cleared about twenty thousand dollars, he thought that his dear wife deserved a nicer place to live, and consequently bought an elegant eight room stone front house on the "South Side," which was in a very aristocratic neighborhood.

In large cities, families "come and go" unnoticed by their nighbors, in fact a family may live a year in one place and not know his next door neighbor's name, and such was the case with Wilbur Mattingly and his family, as they were content to live to themselves, as this was a man and wife truly in love with each other.

Wilbur's business kept growing and his bank account kept getting larger and larger, and his dear wife grew more handsome as the years rolled by.

Within four short years Wilbur's bank account had climbed up to the snug sum of twenty-five thousand dollars, and his home was paid for, therefore he bought a fine carriage and a "span" of fine matched horses. As soon as this happened "the neighbors" pricked up their ears, and Wilbur Mattingly became known at once as the "rich manufacturer," and "Society's" vulgar crater began to yawn for its "rake off."

Two darling girls had blessed the happy marriage of this happy family, and both of these little girls

(7)

inherited the classic beauty of their mother. They
were the delight of their parents, and as soon as
society on the "South Side" realized that Wilbur
had money these children were "petted" by all the
neighbors, as Mrs. Mattingly always dressed them
with exquisite taste.

To Mr. and Mrs. Mattingly's surprise they soon
began to receive invitations to all the social functions on the "South Side" and it was not long until
the "Mattingly's" were considered the "proper thing"
and the male population who furnished the money
to back these "Social Hells" began to "Palaver"
over Mrs. Mattingly, in fact she was the most "noticed" woman in the neighborhood, as she was indeed the most beautiful in that section of Chicago.
Hundreds of families in South Chicago will readily
recognize who "Florence" was, as there are many
who live in that section, who remember seeing that
poor woman take her plunge into Chicago's "South
Side Social Hell."

Of course, the "Mattingly's" were compelled to
entertain if they expected to be entertained by their
friends, therefore it was not long until the "Mattingly Home" was thrown open to the unholy tread
of this brigade of Chicago's "South Side" tribe of depraved humanity.

Wilbur Mattingly's father was a Christian gentleman, who sincerely believed that no man or woman
could tamper with intoxicating drinks without having their character lowered to a certain extent, and
Florence's father, he being a Methodist Preacher,
was of course of the same opinion, therefore both
Mr. Mattingly and his wife had imbibed the same
spirit from childhood, consequently were as much
opposed to the use of wines and champagne as their
forefathers, however, as we have previously stated
"Society" endeavors at all times to give her "dupes"
to understand that these ideas are antiquated, as
they tell the uninitiated that these doctrines will
not hold good with the real intelligent, as the intelligent class, such as they claim to be, can "take
it, or let it alone."

Dear reader, this argument has been used by the
Devil since the "fall of Adam" and will be used just as
long as the world stands and fallen humanity will always prove the absurdity of such arguments, for it is a
certain fact that you can not stand out in the rain
without getting wet, neither can you thrust your
hand into filth without her grime attaching itself to
your person, and neither can you partake of liquor
in the manner that society does, without creating

an appetite, either to love it or to love its effect, and
one is as destructive as the other.

Mr. and Mrs. Mattingly, when they first began to
attend these social functions, utterly refused to touch
wine or champagne, stating that they had a family
and did not believe in doing something they would
be pained to see their daughters do in after years,
but society only "tittered" and replied that it was
their early training that made them have these old
"fogy" ideas, and further stated that they would soon
learn to be "up-to-date" and oh! how true! how true
did society's prediction come true, for in a very short
period of time Mrs. Mattingly was tampering with
this hellish stuff and eventually persuaded her husband that there was no harm in drinking wine in a
moderate way, and she very soon persuaded him to
join her also in her downward march that as sure
leads to destruction as "sparks fly upward."

The next social gathering that was given at Mr.
and Mrs. Mattingly's home was amply supplied with
"society's drug."

Mrs. Mattingly's appetite for strong drink grew
with wonderful rapidity, in fact her husband within
a short time would entreat her to abstain from its
use, as she had began to partake of it in such quan-

tities that she would become under its influence, and had very very often within the past few months attended these gatherings to return home in a maudlin condition.

This had began to worry Mr. Mattingly to no little extent, and he would entreat his dear wife to let it alone, but to no avail, for as time went by he could gradually see his dear wife, the mother of his two darling children, sinking, sinking, sinking deeper down into the quagmire of social ruin.

She had made the plunge and it seemed to Mr. Mattingly that no earthly power could extricate her from the debasing influences of Society's grasp, consequently he lost interest in his business and within a short time he was traveling upon the same road with his wife, hand in hand, down, down, down the slippery and slimy road that so soon terminates at the station, known all over the civilized world as the "Gutter" or last and lowest stage of the drunkard.

Within an incredibly short time the auctioneer's red flag hung from the front door of the manufacturing plant of THE MATTINGLY MANUFACTURING COMPANY, and its contents, assets and good name of this once prosperous factory, was sold under the "Sheriff's hammer" to satisfy the creditors of this once prosperous concern.

The proceeds of the sale amounted to a few thousand dollars more than it required to satisfy his debtors, and this amount was turned over to Wilbur, which he and his wife soon squandered in riotous living, however at this time they had sunken so low in the scale of humanity that they had to seek a lower grade of Society than the one they had been used to moving in. In a short time this money was spent and a mortgage of $7,000 was placed upon their beautiful home in South Chicago, and within two years from the time this mortgage was placed, this once happy home was sold to satisfy the mortgagee, and Wilbur and Florence moved from there into a semi-respectable part of Chicago without hope of the future, as their ambiton was gone and all they cared for was to appease that devilish appetite caused by mingling with what the world calls "respectable society."

They still had their furniture, but piece by piece this furniture was carted off to the pawn shop in order to get "rum" and provisions to exist upon, and within twelve months the handful of furniture still remaining in their possession was set out upon the street because Wilbur Mattingly, the once prosperous manufacturer could not pay the pitiful sum of $7 per month to an exacting landlord.

Neither Mr. nor Mrs. Mattingly's family knew of the awful condition of them and their children, as they had never written them they were nearing the last "eddy" that would whirl them into the arms of cold charity.

The two little girls had grown by this time into almost womanhood, and they, too, from the example set by their father and mother had begun to partake of this hellish drug called "rum" and their associates were of the lower class of humanity, for by the time they had grown to womanhood their father and mother had reached a very low plane in the social world, consequently the influences that these girls had thrown around them were anything but first class, so you will see that these girls did not have to go very far before they struck the lower strata of humanity.

Nothing but starvation stared this family in the face, so Wilbur Mattingly screwed up his courage to the point of desperation and wrote his father regarding his circumstances, but in the meantime both his father and mother had died, therefore he could secure no help from that source.

Florence, his wife, stoutly refused to write her parents, stating that she did not propose to disgrace

herself and family and then place a dark shadow
upon the lives of her parents, but eventually her husband prevailed upon her to write her parents and
state their circumstances, which she did and within
forty-eight hours her dear old father, bent in years,
called at their city "Hovel," which is   the   lowest
"Hovel" on the earth, as no dwelling in the country
can be so low as the home of the needy in a large
city.

Her father came and took the entire family back
to his humble home in the State of Wisconsin. However, Florence, his once beautiful daughter, could not
be satisfied without "drink" as her appetite had been
so deformed, as it required daily a certain amount of
liquor to appease it, and without it she was the most
miserable woman on earth, and such was partially
the case with her two daughters, as they had culti-
vated their appetite for this damnable drug until
they too were following the footsteps of their mother
with wonderful rapidity.

Wilbur Mattingly within ten days from the time
he reached his father-in-law's little home in Wisconsin, was killed by a locomotive while in a drunken
stupor near the outskirts of the town, thus ending a
life which blossomed and flourished in its early man-

hood as the bay tree but so soon came to an untimely and disgraceful end at the hands of "Society" in South Chicago.

Florence and her two daughters remained with their father a short time, but that everlasting, eternal craving for strong drink could not be appeased; therefore while her father was filling one of his country appointments, Florence and her two daughters sold a part of her dear old father's furniture, and secured money enough to go back to Chicago, and have a few dollars left after arriving there.

Florence Mattingly still lives in Chicago. Did we say Live? Ah! no. She only exists, as her haunts are the vilest places on earth, but she still has, a-way down in the silent recesses of her heart, a small spark of womanhood left; however, you have to gently fan that spark before you can revive it to a sufficient degree to realize that there is a vestige of womanhood within that blear-eyed, sunken form, which was once considered the most lovely woman in the State of Wisconsin, and who was the idol of a loving and devoted husband.

I was told of Florence Mattingly's fate and spent a great deal of time in the slums of Chicago, trying to locate this depraved mortal, in order to get a state-

ment from her, as I believe her history is one of the
saddest that has ever come under my observation.

I found her, poor thing, in a drunken sleep on the
fourth floor of a tenement house in that district of
Chicago, where it is dangerous for a man to walk in
broad daylight. I asked her for a recital of her miserable life and she railed out, in her drunken stupor
and used language that would cause the vilest to
blush, but I remained with her until I fanned that
little spark of womanhood into a flickering flame,
and thereby secured from this poor miserable woman
a tale which would bring tears to the most hardened
wretch on the face of the earth.

After I obtained her life's history I then visited a
number of persons who were acquainted with her in
her palmy days, and they verified her statements in
every detail.

The reader has her life in this chapter up to the
time that she and her daughters left her father's
home in Wisconsin, and returned to Chicago, and
the remainder of her existence up to the time I
found her piled upon her filthy bed of rags, but from
this time on I will repeat what she told me in her
own language, word for word, as I have in my possession her life in her own hand writing.

Her terrible story follows with the exception, however, of her early girlhood, and her married life, and up to the time that her father took her back to her home in Wisconsin.

"No wife in the great city of Chicago nor in any other land where man dwells, ever loved her husband as I loved mine, and I do not believe that any woman was ever loved by man, as Wilbur Mattingly loved me.

"We were blessed with prosperity and had plenty of money and thought it would add to our happiness to enter society, but oh! that miserable mistake, as it haunts me day and night, only when I am lost to the world on account of this terrible thing called drink.

"I am to blame for the downfall, not only myself, but my husband and both of my darling girls, as I alone was the one that forced Wilbur Mattingly to take his first drink.

"The society ladies of my neighborhood had laughed at me and goaded me for not allowing him to enjoy himself as other men did, and further stated that so long as I kept him "under my thumb" as I was doing, that just that long my pleasures would be limited, as there was nothing that made man so congenial as a few "Glasses of wine."

"I knew that I could never induce Wilbur Mattingly to take the first drink without I set the example, therefore I resolved to set that example, which has lost me my husband, my children, my friends, my fortune, and above all has lost me my reputation and has sunken me so deep down in the scale of humanity that I do not believe God Himself, if I should come as a repentant child, would recognize me.

"I realized that I was gliding away from my early training: I realized that I was slipping away from respectability; I realized that I was floating down the stream that leads to that eternal chasm, called shame, but I had no power to save myself, as my desire for strong drink was so uncontrollable that I was utterly helpless.

"Society clapped their bejewelled hands when I showed my depravity. The women who called themselves ladies and leaders of Society gave me to understand that I was just as much thought of after I had taken my first drink, yea, after I fully realized that I was getting near the precipice of destruction, and laughed at me when I bewailed my awful condition.

"I was a true wife for a long time after I began

my downward course, that is I mean I was true to
my husband, and he died believing that I had always
been true to him, but oh! My God! how deceived he
was, for I had ruthlessly thrown my marriage vows
aside many, many times with that profligate herd of
Devils who were the arch instigators of my downfall, but poor Wilbur never surmised how low I had
sunken, as I was cunning enough to keep that part of
my shame from him, but my two darling daughters
who were at that time young women, and who of
course looked to me, their mother, as their guide,
learned of my perfidy, and my infidelity to my husband; however, I cautioned them, under no circumstances, to let their father know this.

"Of course they considered what mother would
do, all right, thus you can see how easy it was for
them to follow in my footsteps, and justify their
actions by saying that "mother taught it to us."

"Oh! that I had been born barren, I would then
have only the sins of my own to answer for, but tied
around my soul is the destruction and ruin of my
own darling children, which would sink my soul so
far in hell that the most degenerate inhabitants
thereof would shun my society.

"Did you ask where Mamie and Ethel were? Oh!

Go to the records of the Police Court or to the
Ledger of some House of Prostitution, and there you
may learn, as I have not seen them for seven years
and I hope that I may never lay eyes upon them
again, for I realize that their downfall is my fault,
consequently I could not bear to look upon the eternal
wrecks of these two dear girls, who might have been
today loved and respected wives and happy women.

"You ask me if I believe that there are many un-
faithful wives in this wreckless society gang? Ah!
could you read the history of seven out of every
ten, you would find pages so black with immorality
that you would begin to believe that the female world
was a band of prostitutes. But oh! I know it is not
so, as the women who keep themselves untainted
from Society's filthy touch are the women who have
made, and will make the true and loving wives for the
honorable men of this country.

"You ask me why I do not 'straighten up' and re-
form? Ah! why do you not ask me why the Chicago
River does not flow backwards? It would be just as
easy for this river to flow up stream as it would be
for me to steer this poor polluted mortal craft out into
the pure waters of womanhood, as I have created an
appetite that is so depraved that nothing but death
can quench its cravings."

Reader, society has not only dragged this poor mortal down to the lowest level of humanity, but this same "demon eyed harlot," wrecked the life of this loving husband and destroyed every earthly prospect of these two daughters, who might have made loving wives and respected citizens, but for the cankerous touch of this "Society gang" of schemers of the fashionable "South Side" in that great western metropolis, Chicago.

Wives, mothers, daughters, fathers, be sure that you keep a close watch upon yourselves, your wives and your daugters, and whenever that gaudy "Chariot of Sin" halts at your door, inform that "She Devil" that this vehicle of sin must never, never again presume to contaminate your wives and your darling daughters by her filthy presence.

A NIGHT IN THE SLUMS OF BALTIMORE – Col. Maple and Rev.Ferguson in a one night tour in the slums of the great city of Baltimore.

Chapter V.

———

What I Learned While on a Visit to That Section of Baltimore Called The "Tenderloin District."

———

Reader, what I am about to relate is not "hear say" as it is what I saw with my own eyes, and heard with my own ears, and no man dare dispute it, and every man or woman who will visit the same section in the City of Baltimore, or for that matter of any other large City in America, or any other country, will see the same sights, and if they make inquiries they will have the same pitiful tales of misery told to them.

Many believe that the majority of "Fallen women" come from what "Society" would call the "lower walks of life," which is true as Gospel. But bear in

mind, that the "lower walks of life," in my judgment,
and in the judgment of every intelligent man and
woman who have ever investigated and interested
themselves in behalf of these poor miserable creatures, will soon learn that the "lower walks of life"
does not mean the children of poor parents, or the
children of the country farmer, or those who must
labor for their daily bread, but the "lower walks of
life" are crowded in my humble judgment with the
wives, sons and daughters of the rich old "humbugs,"
and often, yea, very often, that old "rich humbug" is
upon that same "lower walk," for he considers that
he can do as he pleases, as well as his family, and
it will be all right, simply because the "old rascal"
has money. Thus the reader sees that when the
"rich" talk about people in the "lower walks of life,"
they mean the humble farmer who tills the soil; the
honest mechanic, or the industrious servant girl, but
they more often refer to their own "ilk," for if any
part of humanity can get upon a "lower walk of life"
than these "drunken" rich old reprobates, and their
society families, they will be compelled to crawl
under hell to find that "walk."

By way of explanation I beg to state that my poor
Aunt's money she left me, a few short years before

this chapter was written, was getting down to a very small part of itself, as I had "wasted it in riotous living," for I did not have sense enough to keep away from that gang of society leeches; however, I was fully convinced what they were, but there was a fascination that drew me near that awful vortex, if not directly in it, however, I awoke to society's awful practices just barely in time to miss the rapids of destruction, and upon coming to myself and realizing that my fortune had slipped almost entirely through my fingers, I made up my mind to spend the remainder of my days in endeavoring to warn mothers and fathers, sons and daughters of this country, of the awful danger of "Society's withering touch."

I had come to believe from what I had already seen of what the world was pleased to call "best Society," that if the "worst Society" was any more depraved than what was claimed to be "best Society" that it must be a deformed "hag" indeed.

I knew what "best Society" (?) was, as I had been there, and beheld it in all its glory, and now I desired to see what the world called "worst Society" was, for I could not see how that "worst Society" could be as bad as what I had been told was "best society."

I had learned to despise city life as it is all "a sham," and I dreaded to make another trip to any large city, but after leaving the home of Mrs. Frankness whom we mentioned in a previous chapter, I concluded to go to Baltimore and stay long enough before retiring to my "Hoosier" home, to learn what the "tenderloin section" was like.

I stopped at a private boarding house as I did not care to be recognized by any of "Society's gang," and well I knew should I put up at any leading hotel in Baltimore, that I was almost certain to "run up against" one or more whom I knew while I was spending my Anut's money with a lavish hand.

I arrived in Baltimore about 8 o'clock one evening, but was too tired to make the "rounds" that night, so retired early, but about nine o'clock next evening, which was Thursday, I dressed in plain country fashion, and sallied out upon my first "slumming expedition," that is the first one where the inhabitants willingly admitted that they were actually that class; however, before midnight I learned that there was "nothing in a name" as the word "Slum" meant in one place, "houses of Ill Fame," "Dance Halls," "Vulgar Shows," and many other disreputable things, which existed, and did not care if you called them "Slums," while the "incubators" or mothers of these "slums" called themselves "Society."

Now don't believe for a moment that there is no respectable "Society" for if you do, you are mistaken, but you will know it when you see it.

If she jingles her wine glasses at every gathering, you can rest assured that if she is at that time respectable, the dark shadow of shame is stealthily creeping closer each moment, and it will not be long until that "black winged vulture of scandal" will soon ruthlessly flap her bony wings over the prostrate form of some poor deluded miserable "Mother's darling," who has been enticed by society to sacrifice her good name to the lust of man's depravity.

- During the day previous to my night of "Slumming" I had become acquainted with a young man who was stopping at the private boarding house that I was stopping at, and learned that he was "studying for the Ministry." He was a bright, open-faced young fellow, therefore I thought I could trust him with my mission, as I was a little anxious to have some one go with me on this "Slumming" expedition, so I introduced myself, and explained why I desired to make the trip through the "Tenderloin" district of Baltimore, and after considerable coaxing and persuasion

I obtained his consent to accompany me; however, he was not anxious for the trip as he was a little dubious of the propriety of it, but after I had fully explained to him that I had spent nearly a million dollars with what was termed the "upper crust" of society, and found it so "rotten" and that I expected to spend the small remainder of my Aunt's million in trying to expose "Society's" depravities, I had no trouble in getting him to go with me.

About nine o'clock we arrayed ourselves in clothes which would make us appear as much as possible like well-to-do country business men, as the "Tenderloin" inhabitants, I had understood, were always very anxious to "rope in" the unsuspecting "Country Jake" as they are termed by the "idiotic" city "Fop."

Oh! it makes my blood "boil" to hear any one speak "slightly" of a country man or woman, for I was raised in the "backwoods" of Indiana, and I sincerely wish I had never gotten away from the "backwoods," as then I would not know of the awful deception of the rotten city tribe, who brazenly call themselves "The upper crust."

Well, myself and the "young preacher," whose name was Ferguson, sallied out upon our mission a few minutes after nine o'clock that Thursday night expecting to remain out until midnight or nearabouts.

We first went to the "highest toned" (?) section of the "Tenderloin," which is very "low toned" of course, but everything has degrees, you know, therefore, for the sake of comparison, we will call it the "high toned" part of the "Tenderloin" section.

We hesitatingly walked up to the finest house where the "Red Light" was, on a certain street which we had been directed to, and I could not see a thing different in appearance of that house to the appearance of the hundreds of others I had entered in large cities.

We rang the door bell, and a "maid" answered the alarm, and she looked to me exactly the same as hundreds of other "maids" that I had seen.

She invited us "into the parlor," just as hundreds of other "maids" had done. In a few moments two young ladies (?) glided down the broad stairway, just as I had seen hundreds of other ladies do. They wore very low, yes extremely low-cut dresses, just as I had seen hundreds of "Society" ladies wear. They modestly took a seat in the parlor, just as I had seen hundreds of other ladies do. They remarked that it had been a pleasant day. Just as I had heard hun dreds of society ladies remark.

After a short while these ladies brought in a bottle of wine, just as I had seen hundreds of Society ladies do. They played the piano and sang, just as I had heard hundreds of Society ladies do. They waltzed around the parlor in a crazy whirl, just as I had seen hundreds of Society ladies do. They got "full of booze," just as I had seen hundreds of Society ladies do. They unblushingly became reckless in handling their feet, just as I had seen hundreds of Society ladies become.

I, of course, detected some things that I had never detected in what we call "swell Society," but when you have to sit around a place for an hour or two, to learn the difference between two things, which claim to be exactly opposite to each other, and one is a "something" which every decent person abhors, don't you think that it is about time for one or the other to go out of business?

I had to slip a five dollar note into the hand of a girl they called "Mabel," but the good Lord only knows what her name was, before I could induce her to talk about her past history. About the time I got "Mabel" to talking about her early life, a tall, blear-eyed girl entered the room. Any one could readily detect that this girl had been one of "Society's pets," as an air of actual culture still clung to her, thus you could readily see that at one time she had been one of the "Upper Tens."

She was about "half shot" or properly speaking about half way along the road to a first-class "jag," that is, if there are any "first class jags."

She stopped and talked a few moments to my young friend, paying no attention to me, but she found the young fellow very timid and with a "swagger," strode across towards me. When she had gotten within a few feet of me, she clapped her hands, threw back her head and in a regular "Horse laugh" exclaimed, "Well if here ain't old "Pious Dick."

I knew that she was "dead next" as "Washington Society" had given me the name of "Pious Dick" some time before I had left that band of heathens, because I did not smoke, chew and had never touched a drop of liquor since the night "Ruth Wilmore" started upon her road to destruction.

I did not want to be recognized in a place of this kind, so I says, "Well, 'Girlie,' you have a bad case of the 'Willies' or you have some other poor unfortunate fellow in mind that looks like me."

She came nearer, and looked straight at me, and said, "Well, I might be a little 'twisted in my vision'

tonight, as you are a little bit more gray than you
ought to be, unless your great 'piety' has gone to your
head," and then she laughed a drunken "guffaw" as
though she thought she had said something very
smart indeed. I had, since a very young man, worn
short "Burnside whiskers" as I do still, but this girl
had been standing directly in front, therefore had not
seen the side of my face.

I think she had about come to the conclusion that
she was mistaken as I had gained in flesh in the past
few years, or since I had left "Society's march to
Hell," and weighed at this time a little over three
hundred pounds. I was willing to let "Mabel" keep
my five dollars, for I was anxious to get away from
that place for fear that this girl would recognize me,
as I knew that she had known me at some time, and I
felt quite positive that I had met her in "Washington
Society," however, I could not place her.

She seated herself at the piano and began playing
some frivolous tune, therefore I thought it my chance
to make my escape. I "winked" to my friend and we
started to leave, when to my surprise, as I was pass-
ing by the piano, which I had to do, to reach the
front door, exposing the side of my face to the girl
seated at the piano, she exclaimed, "Ah! Old Man, I

am 'dead next'; if you are not 'Dick Maple,' or, excuse me please, 'Col. Dick Maple,' my name is not 'Dorothy Bigmouth'!"

"Dorothy Bigmouth!" I exclaimed, as I knew she recognized me, therefore it was useless to deny my identity any longer. I at once resolved to turn her recognition into profit, therefore crossed the room and re-seated myself. Dorothy's mind at once cleared from the effects of her evening's dissipation, so it seemed that a remorseful conscience was gnawing at her every heart string. I turned to "Mabel," the girl who had my five dollars, and told her to keep it, and also gave her to understand that our conversation could be considered closed, as I considered "Providence" had placed "Dorothy Bigmouth" in my hands that night.

We seated ourselves in the far corner of the room, neither having spoken another word since Dorothy had recognized me, as it seemed that this poor girl was indeed embarrassed and heart-broken, as I imagined the scenes of her past social victories, in a panoramic view floated before her eyes, and I know that I was embarrassed for two reasons. First, and the greatest was, because I was found by some one who had previously known me, in a house of this char acter, and the second reason why I was embarrassed was, because I had found "Dorothy Bigmouth" claiming this house of "ill fame," as her home.

Eventually I turned to her, and says: "Dorothy, what in the name of God ever brought you to this?" She as coolly as though she was answering a business question simply remarked, "Fashionable Society."

I asked her how long she had been following this wicked life of vice, and she replied by asking me how long it had been since I was in Washington Society, and stated that she was jut as good now as she was then, with the exception, however, that she was then trying to captivate a husband who had money, but now was trying to captivate money with no thought of securing a husband, for she well knew men who are desirous of becoming husbands never rang the door bell of houses on this street to find wives.

I asked her to give me the cause of her downfall, and she remarked, "Col. Maple, it is a business proposition with me now, as both my Mother and Father are dead, and if you want a history of my life, you must pay me for my time."

I handed her a crisp $20 bill, which she took, and thanked me for it, and I believe she was the most grateful mortal I had ever seen, for she told me that this was the first honest and honorable dollar that she had ever earned in her life.

As near as I can remember Dorothy Bigmouth's story of shame was, that her father had been appointed to some office within the gift of the President of the United States, and had moved to Washington, taking his entire family along.

While in Washington Dorothy's mother's father died, leaving her several thousand dollars, which they used in immediately entering "Society." To this Dorothy attributed the beginning of her downfall, and stated that her mother was an indulgent mother and could see no wrong in anything that her children might do, and endeavored to grant every request made by them.

She stated that she had two brothers, and she being the only daughter, of course, she was petted and every demand she made was obeyed.

"I dressed well, in fact my only thought was in 'finery,' and I attracted about me a score or more of unprincipled and unholy men, believing at that time that their intentions were only those of a gentleman, but how sadly I was mistaken. I drank wine as all society does, you know, and whenever a woman drinks wine at all, and makes a practice of drinking it in small quantities, she soon will be drinking it to excess, and whenever she drinks it to excess, she will sooner or later lose control of herself; as wine, Col. Maple, you know as well as I, is the Devil's best weapon to arouse the passion of either man or woman. My two brothers are still living, but I have sunken so low, that neither of them will recognize me nor allow me to come about them, they both being married and have families, and I do not blame them in the least for it, as I am not a fit character to mingle with decent people.

"My father and mother both died, our money was gone, and there was nothing left that I could see for me to do but to practice in an open and above-board manner what I had for years practiced in Society, while moving in what Washington called 'First class Society.'

"Oh! I hope Colonel Maple that some time I may be able to extricate myself from the terrible plight that I am in, and if I had such men as you to talk with, and pure women to mingle with, I sincerely believe that within a very short time I could step out and be as pure a woman as it is possible for a miserable soul like me to become.

"But it is folly for me to think of it, for where could I go and find employment, as I have no one to refer to, for the ones who were once my friends, or claimed to be my friends, would not recognize me, much less recommend me to some one who would give me a chance to make an honest living, and start life anew."

She wound up by saying that she wished that she could die, and further stated that it would not be long until the "Potter's Field" would have another victim, as she did not propose to live this life of degradation very much longer.

She concluded her story by saying, "that her's was not a new story, as she could go into that part of Baltimore, and especially that street termed 'the best houses' and nine out of every ten of their inmates had had exactly the same experience as she."

She further stated that the inmates of "viler dives" had had the same experience, with this exception, however, that they had not started so high up in Society's deceitful realms, therefore the fall had not humiliated them as much as it had her and the other inmates of what this "Tenderloin" section called "swell houses."

I asked Dorothy if she would go with me to a

(9)

number of other houses in order that I might get the testimony of other individuals, and informed her that I was willing to pay for the information, provided that the inmates did not care to unfold their tale of misery without compensation.

She refused to give her consent to do this, stating, she felt absolutely certain there were a number of "girls" on that street who would recognize her, as she had already met two different ones whom she had known in Washington, and further stated that she did not care to let those whom she once knew, learn that she was following the life that she was, nevertheless these other girls were following the same life. Thus I was led to believe that there was still hope for Dorothy Bigmouth, as she still retained a sufficient amount of modesty to hold out to herself the hope that "some day" she might escape the awful life she was living.

I did not feel like urging this girl to go with me for fear that it might help to more completely callous her already sin cursed soul.

I asked her if she knew what became of Clara Middlewest, and she told me the history of Clara's downfall, which was exactly the same history as hers, only that Clara Middlewest fully realized the awfulness of her condition and immediately, both she and her mother tore loose from this gang of "Social Pirates" and returned to their Missouri home, and Dorothy informed me that Clara Middlewest was at that time the wife of a prominent business man in the State of Missouri, and was respected and loved by all who knew her, for Clara's mother had given the neighbors of that section of Missouri to understand that this little baby which so mysteriously entered the home of the Middlewests, belonged to her own sister, who had died in the State of Minnesota and who Mrs. Middlewest had taken to raise, therefore you see, that by the helping hand of her mother, Clara Middlewest was snatched from an almost certain destruction, and enabled to at least live a part of her life as a true and virtuous woman. However, dear reader, do not "tempt fate quite so far," as there is but one case out of every ten thousand that terminates as that of Clara Middlewest, consequently you are tampering with almost certain destruction when you trust yourself in the hands of fickle and ungodly "Society."

I bade Dorothy "good night," and with her cheeks wet with tears of repentance, she promised me that she would take the twenty dollars that I had first

given her and the twenty dollars that I slipped into
her hand when I bade her "good night," and would
endeavor to leave at once that "Mansion of Shame."
However, I cannot inform the reader whether she did
or not, as from that time to this day I have never
heard of Dorothy Bigmouth.

By way of explanation, I would like to state to
the reader that Dorothy Bigmouth was the daughter
of the lady who so "graciously" gave me the "Carriage Ride" in order to tell me that Clara Middlewest
had been "retired" from Society, which I related in
a previous chapter.

I and my "young preacher" friend was about
ready to give up our "Tenderloin Expedition" and return to our boarding house, as we had learned enough
in this short time to thoroughly convince us that the
"lower walks of life" were crowded with lost and
ruined mortals from the "upper walks of life," and
I did not desire to listen to the awful stories of these
poor, wretched girls, as their tales of sorrow and
shame invariably date back to fickle and abominable
examples set before them by individuals who claim
to be "Society leaders."

We concluded to walk down the street its full
length, more for curiosity's sake than anything else,

my young friend getting on one side of the street
and I on the other, and making notes of all that we
saw. On my side of the street I counted 48 of these
houses, and on his side he counted 39, making a total
of 87 elegant houses, situated in the great city of Baltimore and used for this purpose, and these eighty-
seven houses, bear in mind, were considered "swell
houses of Vice," or, properly speaking, the dumping
ground for "Elegant Society's Dupes."

. Suppose that these 87 houses contained but six
inhabitants each, you have a total of five hundred
and twenty-two girls who were once the pride and
joy of a mother's and father's heart, and the loved
and petted sisters of some brother's affection, and
the courted sweethearts of some honorable young
man.

I have put the number very low when I say five
hundred and twenty-two, as these houses contain
nearer ten or fifteen inmates each, instead of six, and
such is the case in every large city in the land, so
the reader will see with but very little figuring that
Society not only builds these "Gilded Mansions of
Shame" with the heart's blood of bereaved mothers
and the blackened character of the darling girlhood
of our land, but she fills them with these poor mortals

who are compelled to remain in this atmosphere through life, simply to gratify that "demon eyed harlot" that so innocently parades herself as the "upper crust" of Society, and who has the brazen audacity to set the example for the masses. And be it said to the everlasting shame of the masses that they endeavor in every conceivable manner to pattern after this despicable and immoral class of God's creatures.

After tramping down the length of this awful street, crowded upon each side with these houses of "vice" and after noticing in particular one large elegant mansion upon the side of that of my young preacher friend, we concluded to turn back and learn, if possible, why this house was more elegant than all of the others.

This "Mansion of Shame" set back perhaps fifty feet from the street, its lawn was kept in perfect trim, in fact, one who did not know the character of this street would suppose that this house belonged to one of the "aristocrats" of the City of Baltimore.

We noticed there was an alley that ran along by the side of this house, and we also noticed that there were a number of elegant carriages standing down this alley, which we could not account for, so we plucked up all of our courage, and marched up to this "Carnal House of Degradation" and rang the door bell. The door was opened, this time, however, by a "Butler," dressed up in regular military style, his clothes being covered with gold braid, that would lead any one to beieve that he was an attache of some foreign prince. When this door opened we could gaze down the magnificent hall, and I never beheld a more elegantly furnished hall in all of my travels, and I have mixed and mingled with some of the richest and most aristocratic people in the United States, to say nothing of other countries.

This "Butler," or "Flunky," if you please, made a bow that would do credit to the subject of any monarchy, bowing to the greatest despot that ever reigned.

This was so different from our reception at the other house where "Dorothy Bigmouth" stayed, that I was actually led to believe that perhaps we had gone beyond the limits of this "Tenderloin" district and perhaps had wandered into the home of one of the "aristocrats" of the great City of Baltimore. However, my delusion was soon brought to an abrupt end, for this "Flunky," with another bow, says, "Gentlemen, step in and be seated," at the same time pushing a very elegant, upholstered chair towards each of us.

I knew that he would not have invited us in had it been the house of an "aristocrat," as, of course, he would have had to have known us personally or else seen his "master" or "mistress" before permitting us an entrance.

We were seated, he closed the door, and says, "Gentlemen, you will please give me your cards," at the same time pushing under our nose an elegantly engraved gold card tray.

My friend remarked that he had no card and the "Flunky" replied "that no gentlemen could 'See the Ladies' without first sending in his card."

i had become very much interested in the proceedings and was determined, if possible, to learn the difference between this "House" and the other one that we had previously entered. I, therefore, handed him my card which read, simply, "Dick Maple," and after the word "Dick Maple" I wrote with lead pencil "and friend."

This gaudily attired "nothing" with a bow, disappeared and within a few moments he reappeared and with another military bow and salute says, "The Ladies will be glad to see you; walk this way gentlemen." We followed this "monkey" down this long hall and were led into a large reception room, furnished in style that would make an oriental king green with envy, as I frankly acknowledge that I had never before nor since beheld such grandeur.

There were no "Ladies" (?) present, when we first entered, but within a very short time, two elegantly dressed "Harlots" enterd, and lo and behold one of these deliberately walked up to me and with outstretched hands and seemingly without the least particle of embarrassment endeavored to greet me as a friend and remarked, "Col. Maple, I am so glad to see you."

I knew she must have known me somewhere, or she would never have called me "Colonel," as my card read simply "Dick Maple."

I could not call to memory where I had ever met her but she soon refreshed·my memory by saying that she was the wife of an official, who I very well knew from the State of New Jersey.

I asked her in the name of Heaven what she was doing here, and she coolly replied that she was on a visit to a friend in Baltimore while her husband was on a business trip out in the State of Oregon.

I was astounded beyond expression, and said, "When did you and your husband separate?" She, as calmly remarked as before, without seemingly one tremor of embarrassment in her tone, "Why, Colonel, we have not separated, as I think that I have the best husband on earth, and I and my friend only called here this evening to have a little fun."

I was disgusted and heart broken, and at once remarked to this fair "she imp of hell" that I had beheld vice as I thought in its lowest form, but this was the cap sheaf, and, I presumed, the last and lowest step that mortal could possibly take."

I boldly remarked to my friend, Rev. Ferguson, that I would not remain in this house another minute, under any circumstances, as I would expect a just God to strike me dead, should I do so, and at once left this "awful palace of sickening shame."

We had almost reached home, before either of us gained our speech, and we both arrived at the conclusion that there could not possibly be a lower step that mortal woman could take.

It makes me heart sick to relate this sad story.

On the following day I made inquiry from some of the best people in Baltimore, and learned that this "gilded mansion of shame" was the meeting place of "married ladies" (?), who had broken the sacredness of their marriage vows.

I am quite sure that this "married harlot" thought

at first, that I was a frequenter of such places, but had never discerned my real mission, for I am quite sure had she known my mission, she would have been the last person on earth to have shown her depraved face.

I left Baltimore as soon as possible, and I have never remained in any large city longer than it was absolutely necessary for me to perform the business that I was upon, and I warn every man and woman who desire to be ladies and gentlemen, as God expects them to be, that if they are forced to live in a large city, in the name of God look well to the fabric of your manhood and womanhood, and the society of your children, whom God has blessed you with.

WOMAN—"The noblest work of God."

Chapter VI.

Woman.

WOMAN! What a word! No language on earth would be complete without it. Woman, man's mother! Woman! Man's hope, and without her, this old earth would roll into eternity without the melody of God, as this magic word, "Woman," makes the world akin, and her inhabitants brothers.

The world pays homage to "pure womanhood," and without her pure society, the earth would become a barren waste without a single oasis.

Where would you look for "pure womanhood?" Would it be at Society's shrine? Would it be where strains of rich music float from vaulted and frescoed ceilings of the mansion of the rich? Would you halt at the door of the fashionable ballroom, and inquire if "pure womanhood," which is the greatest treasure on earth, dwelt there?

Would you visit the mansions of the millionaire, expecting to find this, the greatest and grandest treasure, "pure womanhood?"

I hear a sad voice in the distance, who has had years of association with this class, exclaim in tones laden with the weight of bitter experience. NEVER! We ask this once devotee of fashion and frivolity, why?

Her answer comes like the last sad wail of a lost spirit, NEVER!

Again, we ask why, and again this miserable wreck, who once was the envy of fair women, and the petted idol of deceitful man, answers with a wail more sad than that of a lost soul in hell, NEVER! NEVER, as these places are not the natural habitation of "pure womanhood."

Reader, do not imagine there is no "pure womanhood" to be found in any of these places, for it would be a mistake to think this, as there are many, but few compared to the innumerable host that frequents and abides therein.

The credit is due to "luck," perhaps, more than anything else, that they have retained their purity, as the scheming, hellish ambition of the majority of their associates is, and has been for their destruction, but by the providence of God, as I do not believe much in luck, they have been saved, due more, perhaps, to the prayers of some dear old "mother, who had placed her trust in God," than anything else.

The storm comes and lays her destructive hand upon the virgin forest, and it is twisted and torn from side to side, the sturdy oak is rent from his abode of centuries past, but by the side of this sturdy oak, whose roots have penetrated deep into the earth, stood the frail and delicate elm, which was not touched by the storm's fury. We stand amazed at such a spectacle, but can not account for it, and can only exclaim, "God's ways are most wonderful to behold."

So it is with that frail and tender girl, who places herself within reach of "Society's whirlwind" and withstands the tempest of "lust's fury." She may emerge from that furious tornado unscathed, but what a miraculous escape she has had, as all about her are strewn her sisters, torn and bleeding from the effects of this "Social hurricane."

Both moral and profane history teaches us that "Home" is woman's sphere. What does "Home"

(10)

mean? Ah! Does it mean the unnatural surroundings the rich and giddy possess? Nay! Verily!

Now, reader, do not for a moment believe that we think that to possess money is a crime, as we do not, but we do believe that it is a crime before God to be blessed with wealth and make no better use of it than ninety-nine out of every hundred of God's creatures make use of it in this country. As wealth is a blessing, not only to the one who possesses it, but to the neighbors of that individual, if the possessor uses it as it should be used, but in nearly every instance you will find those who possess riches are inclined to rule with a tyrannical hand, for it seems as though they believed that money makes "manhood" or "womanhood" regardless of what their actions may be.

It is a laudable ambition to strive in an honorable way to be the possessor of money, as man's pleasures are limited only to his exertions to obtain the necessities of life, and we all know full well that money is the basis from which all "artificial" pleasures of life are derived. However, money can not buy the sweet pleasures that come from pure manhood or womanhood, and Oh! how often by the injection of money into the lives of our people does this sweet and noble spirit of manhood and womanhood depart forever.

How often have I seen honorable men and women who were in moderate circumstances lose their honor by having thrust upon them a few thousand dollars by the death of some relative, or by the mysterious whirl of the wheel of fortune.

I would not have to travel far to find a man of this class; in fact, all that I would have to do would be to gaze into the mirror and there behold the image of myself, as I had never been used to money, only in a moderate way before my aunt died, and left me a million dollars, which I squandered in a manner that I am heartily ashamed of. Not simply, because the money is gone, but because I spent considerably over three-fourths of this large amount of money in the company of what the world calls "Society," but, in fact, were nothing more nor less than "Human shams and sharks."

Woman is the subject that we desire to confine ourselves to in this chapter, but we can not take woman and write alone about her, for she is so closely and so securely wrapped about the hearts of mankind that you can not separate them. Therefore, we must travel hand in hand with woman, "the most noble work of God."

If "Society's shrine" is not the natural abode of pure womanhood; if the mansions of the rich, with its vaulted and frescoed ceilings, is not "pure womanhood's" natural home; if the palace of the millionaire is not the natural abiding place of "pure womanhood," then where shall we seek this noble treasure?

Again this tormented spirit who was once the devotee of fashionable society, hovers over our pen and with her bony finger of warning, says "follow me."

We follow this wrecked shadow of what was once a "Society Lady," and we see her depart from the mansion with the vaulted and frescoed ceiling, where strains of enchanting music still reverberate in her ears; she turns her back upon the masion of the millionaire; she turns, and with a warning finger leaves the fashionable ballroom, where the strains of giddy music entice the young, and the glitter of precious stones would indicate that wealth in all of its extravagance and without the love of God, kept time with her sandaled feet to the "Devil's own melody."

Again, this spirit, which was once buoyant and entranced with Society's unholy tread, exclaims, "Follow me."

We behold her as she leaves the recklessness of Society's throng, and takes her flight from the clang

and artificial life of the city, and we follow her to
the humble cottage, where the scent of new-mown
hay and wild flowers float in through the open window, and there, with eyes dilated and wet with bitter tears of remorse, halts before the door of that
humble cottage, where that contented mother sits
and her bevy of children prattle about her motherly
knee, and we hear her exclaim in a voice pregnant
with the despair of ages, "Here is where pure wom
anhood is found."

Ah! mothers, if you have daughters and sons, in
the name of God, keep them with you at your home
and away from the contaminating influence of city
life, which is artificial in every sense, and where
shame and what is called "Social Evil" is considered
by nine-tenths of the city's inhabitants, as a necessity, and where houses of "ill fame" rear their ungodly heads, and practice their "infamous practies"
year in and year out with the officers of the law
cognizant of the fact that they are in existence, and
still they are never molested.

What can you expect of your children when they
are permitted to come in contact, day after day, week
in and week out, year in and year out, with such an
abominable class of degenerates?

The "rich" would have you believe that these houses of "ill fame" are filled from the ranks of the "lower walks of life," but it is not so, and any man who will make the investigation, as I have, will find that it is an abominable lie when that class who terms themselves the "upper crust" of society tries to lay this shame at the door of the poor. However, the very poor in the cities are as vile and depraved as any other class, and it is more easy to detect the miseries of the poor than it is that of the rich in large cities, for they do not have the funds to cover up their shame; but think for a moment if you live in the country, yea, think for a week, and see if you can lay your finger upon a sigle house in your neighborhood or in your county where the "Red Flag of Harlotism" brazenly floats from any house of ill fame.

Ah! No; you can not think of a single house of this character; then you must know that the morals of the country lad and lass are away above par compared with the children who have been brought to manhood and womanhood in the great cities of our land.

Why is it thus? Simply because the lawmakers of these cities are induced by these vagabonds of

God's green earth, to turn a deaf ear to the pleadings of the decent element of our cities by having placed in their unholy hands, money, gathered in by this begrimed class of God's Universe.

It is a historic fact, backed up by all the history of civilized nations, that wherever you bring together in great numbers, people from every "walk of life," and "huddle" them up in close touch within the confines of a limited space, that there you will create an abiding place for immortality, as continually coming in contact and being in close touch with individuals establishes a familiarity, and whenever you establish a familiarity between the sexes, it makes no difference in what clime this happens, you will breed licentiousness, and the rich are no more immune from this malady than the poor, and whenever those who claim to be aristocrats and millionaires undertake to prove the exception, they undertake to only defend themselves, as their argument is fallacious and has been proven time after time an untruth.

The trouble with all of us is, that we are so easily deceived by the gaudy apparel of the rich, and the magnificence of their surroundings; we take it for granted that no taint of immorality could attach itself to these silken garments, and we exclaim,

"Oh! it's the poor who possess all of these besetting sins."

Who is to blame for "Society's arrogant despot-ism? You are; you the humble puppet who grovels at the feet of wealth, and bows to the man or woman who has, perhaps, come into possession of their wealth by dispossessing "honest labor," your only companion, of what rightly belongs to them.

You are to blame for your own miseries, as you never make inquiries as to how this wealth was ob-tained, taking it for granted that it is enough to know they have it.

Where shall we look for the hand that will snatch the rising generations from the awful chasm of im-morality, which threatens the dear sons and daugh-ters of this generation?

Can we expect to find this good Samaritan among the rich and giddy of the cities? Ah! No; then where shall we go to find this anointed angel?

Again, we hear this phantom voice, who was once the giddy butterfly of fashion, exclaim, "Follow me, and I will show you the angelic form of the one for whom you seek."

Again, we follow this once beautiful creature, but now, only the sad-faced phantom of past sad experiences, and behold she leads us again beyond the confines of city life out into the green and balmy meadows of the country, and she halts beneath the cooling shades of the virgin forest and there with a countenance lit up with the burden of her desires tells us that the mothers who bring forth their families away from the turmoil and grime of the city are the ones who must perform this great task.

She gives us to understand that she was once as pure as the morning dew, which clung for a few short moments to the petal of the blushing rose, but who was contaminated by coming in touch with the deceit of city life.

We have followed this female phantom in our mind's imagination and have listened to her warnings, and, lo and behold, she takes on the form of blood and flesh and becomes a living creature.

Her experience makes our hearts sick, as we have wakened up to the dread reality that this phantom we have been following, is still forced to live and endure her terrible remorse, while those who blasted her hopes and sunk her soul in vice still haunt her like a hideous nightmare.

Woman, Oh! what a name! What would the universe do without thee? It is thee to whom we must

look to wash from our Nation's skirts the crimson
and awful sin, placed there by the filthy hand of
society.

We shall not expect this reformation accomplished by the bejeweled hands of society, but we
will look to the modest homes of mothers who raise
their voices to God in humble supplication, and who
will teach their sons and daughters to reverence
"truth," "manhood," "womanhood" and "virtue," and
with this spirit of reverence implanted within the
hearts of the rising generation, the time will soon
come when "Society" will wither and die for want of
"characters to blast," as her past is strewn with the
bleached bones of those who could not withstand her
blighting touch.

Woman! thou art the "Moses" to lead us out of
the wilderness of "Society's shame." Woman! thou
art the angel to breathe the spirit of virtue into
the minds of our daughters. Woman! thou art the
one to plant the seed of manhood deep down in the
hearts of our sons. Woman! thou art the one to smite
the "painted cheek" of the "Society Hag," who would
destroy, not only the bodies of our sons and daughters, but destroy their eternal souls.

Ah! Woman! within thy hand rests the fate and

destiny of future generations. Arouse, ye mothers, from the sunny fields, and vine-clad cottages of the country where nature continually carries the banner of purity, and where the manhood and womanhood of the nations of the earth have first seen the light of day. Woman! well do we know thou art able to perform thy task well; therefore, take into thy hands the destiny of the Nation's young, and with the righteous stroke of virtue paralyze the scarlet and cunning hand of "Society's Hag of Shame."

SOCIETY REBUKED – Jennie Manley of Alabama, with true southern womanhood rebukes society at her Uncle's table in Detroit, Mich. rather than drink wine.

Chapter VII.

The Morals of the Wealthy Compared With the Morals of What the "Rich" Delight in Calling the "Common People."

In this chapter we will undertake to demonstrate to the reader where "strict morality" is found.

If the reader belongs to that class which the rich call "Common People," go at once to the wood shed, or climb up in the hay-mow, and thank God for it; and if you belong to that class who have money in abundance I would advise you to climb ON TOP of the wood shed, or upon top of a tall hay stack and get as near God as possible, and beg upon bended knees for forgiveness, for ninety-nine out of every hundred of this "wealthy gang" have come into posses-

[159]

sion of their wealth through some unfair and ungodly
manner, and some poor wretch has suffered for the
crime.

No man ever became worth a "million" without
he robbed some one to get it, and if he robbed some
one, he is a thief, therefore needs to ask God's pardon,
and also to make restitution at once.

We make the assertion that no man can make a
million dollars in this short life, and do it honestly,
but will qualify this statement, by saying not one out
of every thousand, and it will pay you to keep your
eye on that "thousandth" one, as his actions would
warrant a close watch kept upon him.

We will proceed to demonstrate to the reader that
our statement is true.

Suppose you had been born July the Fourth, 1776,
which would have been over one hundred and twenty-
five years ago, and you had have been employed at two
dollars per day, three hundred days in each year,
since you were twenty-one years old, and had not lost
a day on account of sickness nor bad weather, you
would have within the one hundred and four years
have earned only $62,400.00, or $937,600.00 less than
one million and we have not taken out a single cent
for your living expenses, nor clothes, neither have

we figured that you have been sick nor lost a day in the one hundred and four years.

No man on earth to-day is one hundred and twenty-five years old, and you never saw a man that age; so you will see that while we have given the man one hundred and four years to make the $62,400.00, we have given him at least fifty more years than any man could possibly work, or allowed him $31,200.00 more than he earned, and there are more men getting less than two dollars per day for their work than there are receiving two dollars and over.

If Christ, who was born over nineteen hundred years ago, had been a common man, and had been working three hundred days each year for the nineteen hundred and two years, and getting two dollars per day, he would only have earned $1,141,200.00 without a cent taken out for food and clothing for nearly two thousand years.

Reader, do you suppose that any man can in this short life become a "millionaire," and not have been a thief somewhere along the line?

Oh! Reader, when you learn that a man is worth "half a million," you want to remember the Jew's instructions to his son, "Son, make money honestly, but Jakie, make money," and when you find a man

(11)

worth a "quarter of a million," I would not advise you to believe that every cent was clear of the "blood of extortion."

Why we go into detail relative to this matter, is to more fully fit the reader's mind for what is to follow, for as soon as a man or woman can grasp the enormity of a "million dollars" they can at once see how nearly impossible it is for any man to become a "millionaire" and not be a thief, and if his wealth comes from some act of dishonesty, you may rest assured, that he will suffer for that dishonesty, not only in this world, but in the world to come, and this is why, we desire to draw the attention of the reader to the difference in the morals of the wealthy and the morals of the "common people."

The farmer, the mechanic and all others who labor for their daily bread are the moral class of this country, or any other country, for that matter, and nearly all of the immorality that exists among the "common people" can be traced to the entreaties of the more wealthy, as the rich "fop" beholds a beautiful country lass, and he at once sets his "infamous trap" to ruin her, and she, poor thing, is enticed into his snare by his gaudy raiment and lavish expenditure of money, to be led astray and thrown overboard at the pleasure of the brute who wrecked her good name and forever destroyed her future.

Who is to blame for this? Ah! No one, but your poor old "fool" father and mother, as they have such a craving for money, they are tickled to death to have Mr. Goldtooth drive up in his "swell rig" and take that dear precious daughter out riding, as they want their neighbors to know that "IT" calls upon their daughter. What is the outcome? Nothing only honest Bill Jones and Rube Barlow, who are honest, honorable young men gets "snubbed" for that "thirty-cent fake" with a rich father, who would be afraid to meet a billy goat at night for fear it was the Devil. Bill Jones and Rube Barlow goes to this country lass and ask her what she means by treating them in such a manner, and in their honest, open-hearted way, try to tell her how they love her, and how happy they would try to make her if she would become either of their wives, but to no avail, as she tells them that she can't love them any more since Mr. Goldtooth, with his "fine rig," has come into her life. Oh! what a spectacle, to see these honest lads "turned down" for the smiles of this "creased-trouser dude," who has only one end in view, and that is, the ruin of this country lass, whose father and mother are to blame for her ruin, as they encouraged this "forty-cent" vagabond and urged their daughter on to shame, simply to make "the neighbor girls" feel bad, and, thinking they might entice this son of wealth to their door by forcing their daughter to prostitute her person in the name of wife, not realizing that this "vulgar, unprincipled scoundrel" only desired their daughter's ruin, without the holy thought of making her his wife, as he brags to his city "friends in crime" that he has a "beautiful country girl, who is as sweet as a pink, but as ignorant as a calf," and further says "that she is dead gone on him, and the poor thing thinks I am stuck on her."

He talks to his City friends in this style and winds up by saying that "old bluebeard" (her father) and her dear old mother, whom he calls "Mrs. Woolen Socks," thinks they have as good as got a rich son-in-law, but I'll show them that I'm not of the marrying kind, and if I was, I would not go out in "the woods" after a bride, unless she had more money than I have."

This society "Fop" continues to call upon this country lass, and eventually accomplishes his dastardly purpose by leading this confiding country girl

to believe he loves her, and by making her believe
he intends to marry her, but Oh! does he marry her?
Never. He never had any idea of doing so. He simply uses her for a plaything, to be thrown aside at
his pleasure. Her good name is ruined, whether any
visible signs of his perfidy ever comes to light or not,
as this class of vagabonds never miss an opportunity
to let the world know what they have accomplished,
as they think it smart to have dangling from their
belt, the blighted characters of confiding girls; in
fact, these Devils will congregate together to talk
over their "conquests," as they call their "raids upon
virtue," and the Hyena who can show the greatest
number of "Victories" is considered the greatest hero
in the eyes of his associates.

You know that the "scandal monger" does not
need a "sure tip" to enable him or her to begin wag-
ging their infamous tongues, as they are always
standing around, wide-mouthed, ready to catch in
their ever "spread-sails of scandal" the first "dirty
breeze" from any direction.

Well you know that every neighborhood always
has some "scandal monger" who is ready to "peddle"
the gossip of the neighborhood, and you also know
that this class never allows the ball of contamina-

tion to grow smaller, but upon the other hand, every time they turn this "soot ball of gossip" it grows larger, therefore, a single "wag of a thoughtless tongue" is often the cause of blighting a character.

Well, this young man (apologies to the word man) from the city, who has been calling upon this country girl, becomes tired of his new-found toy, and is ready to seek other characters to ruin, therefore, he "quits," but not before he has started the tongue of gossip, which has disgraced this country lass, and placed a burden of sorrow upon the heads of this old father and mother, which will follow them to their grave.

It matters not whether this "City Demon" has accomplished his devilish purpose or not, he endeavors to leave the impression, nevertheless, for if he failed, his anger is aroused because he did, and he starts the tongue of scandal to "get even," as he calls it.

After this "fiend," which "Society" calls a "good fellow," quits going with this country lass, she wakes up to the realization that she has not only lost him, but also lost the admiration of honest Bill Jones and Rube Barlow, who were at one time rivals for her hand and heart, and who loved her with a manly and pure love, which would defend its idol to the point of death. But, alas, alas, when this poor girl, who has learned the difference between "NOBLE COUNTRY MANHOOD" and "CITY DEMONS," endeavors to entice back to her heart these "honest sons of toil" she learns that they have hearts, which not only love, but also hate with the venom of the deadly and poisonous "rattler."

Did this poor girl expect to walk upon the hearts of those who loved her, and assist others in doing so, and not cause pain? If she did, she awoke from her delusive dream to learn too late, that while "Pure Love" is susceptible to many hard knocks without resentment that there is a limit, and that she has reached it with her country lovers.

She endeavors to explain why she did it, and states that "I only was making a fool of that City Chap," but these country boys, while they may not wear as fine clothes, and their shirt front may be lacking the gaudy diamond, and their hands may not be as soft and white as the city chap's, are MEN of brains, and this explanation does not go very far with them.

They ask this girl why she so ruthlessly trampled upon their hearts when this city "Fop" came upon the scene, and further asks if they had not always acted as gentlemen while in her presence and want to know if she had ever detected the odor of "Rum" on their breath, or the fumes of Cigarettes upon their clothes, or had she ever found anything that did not indicate they were gentlemen?

Her answer was "No."

Then they ask, "why she would endeavor to break their hearts and hold them up to the ridicule of their friends to endeavor simply, to make a fool of this City fellow?" The question is too hard; she can not give a satisfactory explanation, and these country young men, who once worshipped this girl, and either one of whom would have willingly and gladly made her his wife tells her they prefer a woman who "constantly loves" and who does not care to "take a vacation" in order to "make a fool of some one else" and at the same time make "a bigger fool" of the one who would defend her good name with the last drop of his blood. He further tells this poor girl who now sees that she has made a grievous mistake; that he has learned to love another, and will within a short time make her his wife, as she has always been true to him, and never asked a "vacation" to make "a fool of another fellow."

Sadly, this poor girl who has lost her good name at the hands of this dragon of "Society," turns away, knowing full well she has, with her own hands digged her own social grave.

Now, reader, who is to blame for this poor girl's misery? Was it she, herself? No, no; it was that ignorant old father and mother, who were blinded by money, and who thought they could see social prestige, for their daughter.

When this villainous despoiler of womanhood appeared at this country home, seeking the company of this country lass, the father and mother should have warned their daughter relative to the schemes of this class of persons. However, this country father and mother were not altogether to blame, for they had not been warned of the snares which are daily being set by this gang of social pirates, as, of course, society and her rotten gang of cohorts will not warn her "country cousins," and those who know full well of the awfulness of the condition of society, have not manhood and womanhood enough to proclaim it to the world. However, there are many, thank God, who have washed their hands forever of this "Society gang" and who have registered a solemn vow never to again enter that class of society, for well they

know depravity is rampant among this class of God's
unholy creatures.

Reader, the assertion that follows may sound degrading and you may think at first that no father
who loves his children could possibly make the assertion. However, if you will thoroughly digest the
assertion that I propose to make you will see that
it is founded upon principle and upon pure love.

"BEFORE GOD, IF ONE OF TWO THINGS
HAD TO BEFALL ONE OF MY DAUGHTERS, EI-
THER TO BE RUINED IN GIRLHOOD OR YOUNG
WOMANHOOD BY THE CONTAMINATION OF
SUCH A SOCIAL BRUTE AS WE HAVE JUST DE-
SCRIBED, OR BECOME THE WIFE OF THIS
BRUTE AND BE FORCED TO MOVE IN, WHAT
THE WORLD IS PLEASED TO CALL 'SOCIETY,'
AND BRING UP HER FAMILY IN THAT AT-
MOSPHERE, I WOULD CHOOSE THAT SHE LOSE
HER VIRTUE IN GIRLHOOD, RATHER THAN BE
BOUND BY THE SOLEMN VOWS OF MARRIAGE
TO SUCH A 'BRUTE' AND BE COMPELLED TO
REAR HER FAMILY IN THE ATMOSPHERE OF
THIS DEPRAVED GANG OF SOCIAL DEGEN-
ERATES."

Reader, thus you see that the contaminating influences of this thing called "fashionable society" does not confine itself to its own breed, but, like a pestilence, she reaches out with her contaminating hand and despoils the innocent and unsuspecting darlings of our country homes.

When our hearts are bleeding from the terrible laceration inflicted by the cruel hand of society, who shall we blame?

Ah! listen, and I will tell you. You, the fathers and mothers of this land, are to blame, as you have been charmed by the glitter and artificial grandeur of money in unholy hands, and have stood idly by and allowed this "boaconstrictor" of society to coil itself about the pure form of your daughter and drag her down to misery without a protest, and until you realize that a "legal thief," who has come into possession of his millions is just as despicable as the "thief" who can not dodge behind a technicality called "legality," just that long your girls are in danger, for it is an impossibility for parents who have made their "millions" by oppression and robbery and who permitted their offspring to spend their illgotten gains with unstinted hand, to bring up their children to become pure, virtuous sons and daughters, for "like begets like," and the father or mother who trusts their darling daughters with the progeny of society will sooner or later learn they have "sown to the wind," to in turn "reap the whirlwind."

THE DARK SHADOW OF "FASHIONABLE SOCIETY."

Chapter VIII.

Woman's Dress—The Indicator of Her Character.

In this chapter we propose to take up the very delicate subject of woman's dress. However, there would be nothing "delicate" in regard to this subject, was it not for the fact that "Fashionable Society" makes it such.

When the female element of this "Fashionable Society" desires to dress in this unholy fashion they can not complain when decency rebels and points out to her the awfulness of her shame.

The reader may not know how society arrays herself when she attends these social functions, and I am quite sure that if the pure mothers and innocent daughters of this country were to look in upon some

[175]

fashionable gathering, crowded by the devotees of
frivolity, and behold those who claim to be ladies, attired, as they invariably are, in the low-neck dress
and short sleeves, they would exclaim, "Oh! can it
be possible that these women actually believe they
are the modest creatures that God intended them
to be."

1 have beheld with my own eyes, young women
and married ones as well, unblushingly come into
the presence of men with their dresses cut so low
in the back that two-thirds of their backs were exposed and these dresses were cut so low in the front
that it is impossible for me to describe how absolutely indecent they were, but these women, without
one blush of shame, would parade among the male
sex without the slightest hesitancy. Not only would
they unblushingly mingle with the male contingent
of these society functions, but they would permit
these men to waltz with them, which necessitated
them placing their arms about her form, bringing
them face to face with one another and nothing pre-
vented him from gazing down upon her, and beholding her depravity.

The strange part of Society's dress is, that you
never see women with bony arms wearing short

sleeves; neither do you ever behold ladies who move in this class of society wearing these extremely low-cut dresses who have been deprived by nature of well-developed busts, as these "skinny" individuals invariably make "excuses" why they do not attire themselves in this fashion, which is indicative of harlotism.

I heard one lady say to another, "Oh! I always take cold so easy that I can not wear low-cut dresses" or "I have a birthmark between my shoulders or upon my bosom" and many other such excuses, but I have never in all of my association with this "Fashionable tribe" ever heard one of these devotees of fashion act the part of a pure woman and exclaim "I do not wear a low-cut dress because I believe that it is immoral."

When those women made these excuses for being decent, it was all a falsehood, as they did not want to acknowledge that nature had stinted them in the matter of plump arms and well-developed busts.

What can you expect of girls seventeen, eighteen or nineteen years old attending such places and gazing upon what they deem the leaders of society?

Can you expect these girls to be anything but immodest? Can you expect these girls after they be-

(12)

come mothers to implant in their children's minds strict moral principles? No; it is an impossibility, as you can not impart knowledge you do not yourself possess.

These fashionable mothers set this immoral example before their girls when they are in pinafores, by dressing in this half-clad manner themselves, and when these girls grow up into womanhood they array themselves in the same fashion, for they had had their intellect stunted, as it were, from early childhood and never felt that pure womanly flush of shame rush to their brow at beholding such sights, as they were taught to believe that such was the "proper thing."

Oh! What a disgusting spectacle it is to see an old "fat-jawed" "society gusher" strutting around like an overfed goose (I beg your pardon, Mrs. Goose), wearing short sleeves and low-neck dress, and exposing herself to public gaze.

I have heard two or three times in my life some married lady who had not retained her girlish plumpness step up to one of these old, overfed "she devils" and remark, "Oh! Mrs. So and So, you are ten years older than I am and I can not account for your plumpness'," and this old bunch of vanity would make a short "squat" which she intended for a bow, and say "Oh! thank you," and would by way of explanation remark to this younger lady that "perhaps you do not know how to preserve your girlish appearance."

Of course, the other lady acknowledged that she was lacking that information, when this old, "perfumed half-century of sin" would tell her that "she had always brought her children up on the bottle, which was the secret of her retaining her girlish appearance."

I heard this conversation one evening while attending a "social" in the City of Brooklyn, N. Y. I, of course, was not expected to hear this. However, this old lady, with the short sleeves and low-cut dress, had attracted my attention early in the evening, and I could not keep my eyes off of her, not from her plumpness and girlish appearance, by any means, but she was one of the most ridiculous looking creatures that I had ever beheld, arrayed, as she was, as she actually looked more like a comic valentine than anything I could compare her to.

When she and this younger lady were talking, and when she made the remark about "bringing her children up on the bottle," I thought to myself, is it pos-

sible that society will go so far in her wickedness
and in her desire to keep pace with her surroundings, that she will even sacrifice the health of her
children that she may be pleasing in the eyes of the
opposite sex? As it was plain to my mind that the
only reason she wanted to retain her "girlish appearance" was to be noticed by the male sex of Society's followers.

This was the first time in all of my life that I ever
heard any woman openly and unblushingly declare
that she would willingly imperil the health and lives
of her own children in order to appear "girlish" in
the eyes of anyone, and especially a gang of lustful
society degenerates.

Modesty is not an accomplishment, but it is an inborn gift from God, which every true woman has in
her bosom until her corrupt associations destroy her
modesty.

When you rob woman of her modesty you have
robbed her of the greatest jewel, and when that jewel
is gone she has but a short distance to travel before the "tongue of gossip" begins to "wag," and
when this happens, her virtue is called into question,
and when her virtue is destroyed she is an outcast
among man.

Modesty, is woman's shield, and no woman can dress as "Fashionable society" demands and retain the respect of man.

The male sex may demand that she lay aside her "prejudices" as they are pleased to call it, but the demand is made in order that they may glut their lustful eyes at the expense of virtue.

I remember a bright eyed, sunny haired girl, about twenty years of age, from the State of Alabama, who visited her Uncle in Detroit, Michigan, about eighteen years ago. This girl had been raised upon a cotton plantation in Alabama, but who had been raised, thank God, by one of the South's dear "old fashioned" mothers. Oh! that we had a few more "old fashioned" mothers.

Jennie's Uncle was a man of affairs in Detroit, in fact he was what the world would call rich. He was a Southerner by birth but had married a Northern lady, and the daughter of a wealthy Banker in Detroit, who had been brought up to believe that it was all right to go into company half clad.

Her husband made a mild protest at first about her mode of dress, but he was soon silenced by the ironical "titter" of society, as they called him "A Southern Sunday School Boy," so it was not long until he ceased to offer any objections to his wife's immodesty. They never had any children born to bless their home, so they were anxious to have Jennie Manley from Alabama visit them, as she was a beautiful girl with a most beautiful character. Jennie had always been used to plenty, that is plenty in a modest way, as her father was a cotton planter who was considered "well-to-do" by his neighbors.

Jennie's mother was loath to let her go to Detroit as she said she was afraid that the gay society her Uncle and Aunt moved in might put "queer ideas" into her head. However Jennie went, and returned to her father and mother without the taint of "fashionable society" upon her pure womanhood.

When she arrived at Detroit her Uncle and Aunt met her at the Depot that September evening, in their elegant carriage and drove her to their most elgant home in the fashionable part of Detroit, and Detroit you must remember, dear reader, is indeed a fashionable city.

Jennie was dressed in pure white with a pale blue ribbon deftly entwined about her girlish throat, which made her appear a typical country school girl. She was the picture of purity. When they arrived at her Uncle's home, this simple child of an honest

Southern planter, gazed with wide mouthed wonder
at the lavish splendor of her Uncle's mansion. She
was a well bred girl and was above the average in
intellect, but she could not but show her bewilder-
ment at such grandeur.

Her aunt, about ten o'clock says, "Come, Jennie,
I will show you to your room as I know you are tired
after your long journey."

Jennie followed her up the broad marble stairs,
which were a dream of splendor.

Her aunt led her into a room that was draped
in oriental splendor, and says "Jennie dear, this
shall be your room." Her aunt gazed upon this
girlish figure which was as perfect as though it had
been chiseled out of marble by the deft fingers of a
classic workman. She gazed at her, clad in pure
white, with that pale blue ribbon at her throat, and
she declared to me afterwards that she did not believe her dress had cost over two dollars, but declared that Jennie was the most lovely woman she
had ever beheld.

Next morning after breakfast her Aunt said "Jennie, if you don't care I will take you to my dress-
makers and have you a ball dress made." Methinks
that the Angels in Heaven strained their ears to

catch the reply, as a pure innocent country girl was having the first dart of the Devil cast at her by fashionable Society.

Jennie looked at her Aunt and replied, in a pure womanly manner, "I do not go to balls, therefore I need no ball dresses."

Many good resolves have been overcome by the fickle smile of society, so I imagine that even the angels were in doubt whether or not Jennie Manley would cling to her resolution.

Her Aunt says "Well we'll let the matter drop at present, but I think after a while you will change your mind."

The Aunt told me that she could not press Jennie that morning, for she felt that this pure child of the Southland was her master, but why, she could not tell.

Her Aunt informed Jennie that they were to give an entertainment that evening in her honor, and about four o'clock in the evening she remarked to Jennie "that they would drive up to a fashionable tailoress and see if they could not rent a suitable dress for Jennie to wear, for the occasion."

Again Jennie Manley straightened up with all her true Southern womanhood beaming forth from her deep blue eyes and says, "Aunt Mattie, if my own clothes, which my dear old mother and I have made, are not good enough for the people in Detroit, I'll take the train for Alabama this very evening, where I am respected as plain 'Jennie Manley,' and not for my clothes."

Oh! what womanhood. How many girls have we in this country like Jennie Manley?

Aunt Mattie, with tears in her eyes, reached out both hands and drew this girl to her bosom, and says "Oh! if you were my daughter I would be the proudest mother on earth."

Her Aunt told me in after years that this was the turning point of her life.

Jennie's feelings were hurt by her Aunt's requests to "get other clothes," but her Aunt soon gave her to understand that she was sorry she had offended her and assured her that as long as she stayed in Detroit she should wear what she pleased.

Evening came, and about nine o'clock carriages began to arrive, and the double parlors of this grand mansion were thrown open for the occasion, which was given in honor of Jennie Manley of Alabama.

I was on a business trip in Detroit, therefore received an invitation, as I was acquainted with the

Standafords, but I had gone to Chicago that morning, and did not arrive at the Standaford mansion until all of the guests were there.

When I was ushered into the parlors of course this gang of "half dressed" women, and the tribe of "cut away coats" were there, and I was one more to add to this tribe. There were but two ladies in the audience who were not dressed in this immoral manner, and that was Jennie Manley and her Aunt. I was introduced to Jennie, and Oh, what a sweet child of nature she was. She reminded me of a meek violet surrounded by the rank and poisonous weeds of sin.

Wealth was there in all her brazenness. From the ears and throats of this gang of God's brazen creatures called women, flashed precious gems.

Young women were there whose marriage meant thousands to the poor wretch who dared tie himself for life to her, but around this pure and loveable girl from Alabama, clung the main attraction, as purity shone from her girlish face, and her smile was a tonic to famishing society, which knows naught but something artificial.

Supper was announced and served, and of course wine was there in abundance. When Jennie Manley's Aunt passed the vile stuff to her she said, "Jennie, here is a little that is half water, and I made it real sweet."

Jennie looked at her Aunt for a moment with her wondering big blue eyes, and said, "Aunt Mattie, it may be half water, but I do not care to even serve the Devil half way."

As though an electrical button had been touched that connected every man around that table, involuntarily, every one clapped his hands in honest approval, and I honestly believe the manhood of many had been aroused that had never been reached before.

When supper was over not a glass of wine had been touched, thus you see what determination and the will power of purity can do.

After supper the gentlemen retired to the "Smoking Room," while the ladies retired to the parlor, each lady endeavoring to pay homage to this country girl who had refused to obey the dictates of society, and who had with open hand smote the serpent of society without any apologies whatever.

Mrs. Standfaord told me that while the ladies were together that evening one remarked to Jennie "why do you not wear low cut dresses Miss Manley, you have such a lovely form?"

Jennie looked her square in the face and says, "Why do you wear any dress at all?" This society lady says in reply. "Oh, that would be indecent." Jennie Manley remarked to this butterfly of fashion, "that is exactly why I do not wear low cut dresses."

Mrs. Standaford informed me that the evening was a very sultry one, as September you know generally is, but within a half hour from Jennie's stinging retort, every lady had complained of being "cool," and had thrown a cape or shawl over her nakedness.

Mrs. Standaford said, that the remarkable part of the thing was, that not one of these society ladies ever took offense at any of Jennie Manley's straightforward remarks.

Reader, here was a country girl who was inexperienced in what the word calls "knowledge" but she had the courage of her convictions, and kept God in sight at all times.

Several years afterwards, or after I had quit forever "Society's dissipations" I had a talk with Mrs. Standaford and she informed me that she knew of ten different society ladies, including herself, that never again wore a low cut dress, nor served wine upon their own tables, and each of them gave for their reason "that Jennie Manley from Alabama" had taught them a lesson they never forgot.

This pure, blue eyed Southern lass stayed in the City of Detroit several months, but she never forgot her early training, and never missed an opportunity to brand "frivolous society" with the hot iron of justice.

A Mr. Norton who was very wealthy became greatly infatuated with this sweet faced Southern girl, in fact, many "fell at her feet" and sought her "hand and heart," but Mr. Norton was naturally a gentleman until society spoiled him and dulled his manhood, and he endeavored to demonstrate to Jennie that he thoroughly coincided with her in her hatred for the abominations of society, indeed he never missed an opporuntity to try to convince this girl that he had put away forever everything pertaining thereto.

He was desperately in love with Jennie, but halted each time that he thought of asking her to be his wife. Jennie never dreamed that he worshipped her as he did, as she was under the impression that he of course, was looking for some rich elegant lady, therefore when he paid her many attentions she only believed it was done through courtesy to her Uncle and Aunt. However, Jennie was soon convinced differently, as Mr. Norton had gone to both her Uncle and Aunt and laid bare the burden of his heart, and frankly told them that he was desperately in love, but felt his unworthiness to ask that pure country girl to become his wife, as he felt that he was so much below her that it would be a disgrace to ask her to become the wife of such a society renegade.

Mr. and Mrs. Standaford had known Mr. Norton from his youth, and had always found him to be what "fashionable society" called a gentleman. They also knew that he was very wealthy, consequently they were anxious to help the "match" along, so Mrs. Standaford agreed to intercede, or plead his case with Jennie.

One chilly, dreary morning in November Mrs. Standaford called Jennie into the library and drew her chair near the large open grate which burned brightly, and says "Jennie, I have something I desire to speak to you about, and the matter is vitally important to you."

Jennie like an innocent child as she was, turned her great blue eyes to Mrs. Standaford, and says: "Oh, Aunt Mattie, you haven't received any bad news from home have you?"

"No, no, my darling," replied her Aunt, "it is good news."

She began by saying "You know Mr. Norton is an awfully nice young man, and he is one of the wealthiest young men in the city of Detroit, which is saying a good deal, as we have many rich young men here." She continued by saying "Mr. Norton called last evening after you had retired and had a long talk with myself and your Uncle, and begged us to plead his case with you, therefore Jennie I have come to you as an Agent for Mr. Norton to try to persuade you to become his wife."

"To become his wife?" exclaimed Jennie Manley. "I marry that man? Never! I would rather have a mill-stone tied about my neck and be buried at the bottom of Lake Michigan than to be the wife of that man."

Her Aunt held her breath in amazement, as she did not believe this sweet faced Southern girl had so much spirit.

When Jennie had calmed down, Mrs. Standaford wanted to know her reason for branding Mr. Norton "as such a bad man."

"Plenty of reasons," replied Jennie. "He mingles with a class of men that would corrupt the morals of a saint, and with a class of women that are a disgrace to womankind."

"He allows his sisters to appear in public half clad, and drinks wine like the lowest of the earth, and if he does not know better, he is a fool, and if he does, he is a knave and a disgrace to his family, and no man that will brazenly drink wine before a lady, and permit his own sisters to unblushingly exhibit their nakedness in company can possibly make a true husband."

"Oh! Jennie, Jennie" exclaimed her Aunt, "you are too hard on us poor 'Society people,' however I can not but admire you, you dear bunch of honesty."

"Then I suppose I shall tell Mr. Norton that you do not care to marry." remarked her Aunt.

"Tell him that I do not care to marry such as he," hotly retorted Jennie.

"Don't you ever intend to marry, Jennie?" asked her Aunt. "Yes, I do, and in May of next year, and the twenty-second day of May at that," replied Jennie.

"Well, well, if that don't beat my time," declared her Aunt. "You have been here nearly three months and never mentioned it to me before."

"What is your prospective husband like," inquired her Aunt Mattie.

"He is like the Greek Gods of old, only better" calmly replied Jennie.

"Oh, I would so much like to see him, haven't you his photograph?" asked her Aunt.

"I certaily have. Wait a moment until I go to my room and get it." Jennie returned with a cabinet sized photograph neatly wrapped up in pink tissue paper. She unwrapped it with reverential tenderness and handed it to her Aunt, saying as she did so, "there is the man who will be my loved and idolized husband on the twenty-second day of next May, if God spares both of us."

Mrs. Standaford took the photograph from Jennie and beheld the likeness of a smooth faced, broad shouldered, stalwart "son of toil" clad in the garb of a working man, in the act of rolling a bale of cotton on a pair of scales. He was a handsome open faced young fellow, and any one that ever had studied human nature knew that this Southern young man, who was not afraid of toil, was not only handsome but possessed the traits that mature into glorious manhood.

Jennie's Aunt was not slow in telling her that she considered him not only handsome but a noble looking fellow, which seemed to very much delight Jennie.

As the reader perhaps knows, the majority of

(13)

wealthy people are always looking out for their
children to marry some one possessing wealth, therefore it was very natural for her Aunt to ask "What
prospects has your intended?"

"The grandest in the world" exclaimed Jennie,
"As he has character and ambition and loves a girl
that loves him, and if that is not enough prospect
to enable any man on earth to clamber to the dizzy
heights of success, then pray tell me what else is
lacking?"

Early in January of the next year, Jennie Manley
returned to her Southern home without taking with
her a single taint of "Society's contamination" and
on the twenty-second day of the following May, Jennie Manley became the happy wife of Robert Lee
Overman, who is today a respected and honored man
of the State of Alabama, and his wife the happy and
contented wife of a Southern planter.

Reader the history of Jennie Manley and her victory over society is but one out of ten thousand,
for where you find one girl that has the will power
to successfully combat the "She Dragons" and the
"He Demons" of "Fashionable Society" you will find
nine thousand, nine hundred and ninety-nine that
will willingly, and without seemingly a single pro-

test, glide down society's incline of shame, with such momentum that before they know it, they have wrecked their womanhood upon the shoals of society's degradation.

SOCIETY AND MANHOOD – "Choose ye this day whom ye will serve."

Chapter IX.

___

Is it "Fashionable Society" or What They are Pleased to Call "The Common People" That Makes This Nation What It Is?

___

In this chapter we desire to deal with stubborn facts, and we hope to be able to place them so plainly before the mind of the reader that he or she may thoroughly understand what we mean.

In the first place, we desire to ask where the "brain and brawn" of this country comes from?

Does it spring from the lap of luxury? Have the cradles of the millionaires rocked the noblest men and women of this country? Have the wives of the millionaire been the happy mothers of the great

inventors or the great educators of this land? Have
the tender hands of wealth gone out into the wild
forests of America and caused her to blossom as the
rose? Have the daughters of the multi-millionaires
made the sweet-faced wives and lovable mothers of
this country? Have the sons of wealth been found
foremost in the ranks of our armies, fighting the bat-
tles of this beloved country?

Go gather around you from every quarter of the
earth the rich who are found foremost in any of
these glorious undertakings, and you will find but a
small number of this class. However, there have
been a few; but, on the other hand, if you please,
knock at the door of fame and ask the keeper of her
records to bring out his musty journals of time,
wherein is recorded the names of "the common people" who have made America what she is, and you
will find they are legion.

March out from the cities of this country and you
will find humble homes with proud occupants, because of the glorious memory of deeds of greatness
performed by the children of the "common people."

Go to the humble cottages where wealth is unknown and where privation is a familiar caller, and
there inquire for the inventive geniuses of this coun-

try, and they will march before you like a never-ending army of soldiers.

Go to the humble vineclad cottages of this land and knock at their doors and inquire, "From whence comes the statesmen of this land?" And the valleys and hill tops will reverberate with oratory that cannot be surpassed by any country under the shining canopy of heaven.

Go to the country farm houses, which are surrounded with virgin forests and green meadows, and inquire, "From whence do the majority of our inventors come?" and the air will tremble with a mighty rattle of ponderous machinery conceived by the fertile brain of toil.

Stand upon the mountain tops and shout to the four winds of the earth the interrogation, "Where have the divines of this country come from, who have entranced the nations of the earth with their eloquence?" And the answer will come from millions of souls saved by their influences, and the answer will be "from the humble homes of the common people!"

Take the wings of the morning and fly from the eternal icebound shores of the North to the tropical seas of the South, and from where the sun first turns

night into day to where she sinks to rest within the
bosom of the Pacific, and make the inquiry, "From
whence has America derived her greatness?" And
every star will twinkle her answer, every bird will
trill her reply, and every mountain will rumble his
answer "that America could never have been what
she is to-day had it not been for what this demon-
eyed fiend called 'Society' takes pleasure in calling
the 'common people.'"

"Earthly independence causes men to forget
God," and to forget God, turns men into fiends, and
women into harlots.

Take the man of wealth, and all he has to do is to
"wish" and that wish is a reality, as far as earthly
things are concerned. He knocks at the door of
commerce, and if she be stubborn he batters her
down with his cudgel of gold.   a

He desires that which he has not, and by his
mighty treasures of wealth, it is his.

He has been so accustomed to having his desires
gratified that he loses sight of the "Great Giver"
who is the giver of all things.

Wealth has frowned and the world has trembled;
therefore she has learned to believe that no demand
of hers should be disobeyed. Who is to blame for

this arrogance of wealth? Ah! you are, you who are the salt of the earth are to blame, as you meekly permit her to shackle you hand and foot, and lead you to the polls and cast your vote to make laws that govern you. You permit her to fill the offices of the land, and make "injunctions" so binding that you dare not trample upon her unholy mandates for fear of being shot down like dogs.

You, the "common people," who have lavishly filled wealth's lap with all the good things of life, sit idly by or scamper away like children at her bidding, to perform her hellish mission, which means servitude for you and your posterity.

"As you make your bed, so shall ye lie." Then do not whine at the laws of your land when they hang a "mill stone" about your neck, and crush your ambitions, and paralyze your arm when you try to raise it in your own behalf, as you yourself are responsible for your condition.

"Ye fools, by your own hands ye are destroyed." You, or your next door neighbor, are competent to fill the office that you elect wealth to fill. You, "the common people," that "Society" delights to call you, are the voters, but you fail to vote for your own kind, but still persist in "cursing your fate."

Were it not for you, "the common people," want would stalk through the land with ghostly tread. The rivers of commerce would dry up. The ocean grey-hounds would put out their fires. The rumble of the mighty locomotive would cease her rumblings. The buzz of the saw and the clang of the hammer would not be heard. The earth would yawn for the lack of the plow, and misery would take possession of the mansions of wealth.

Ah! manhood, where art thou? Well you know the slurs and insults that are hurled at thee by wealth; then why be truckling slaves to her avarice?

Wealth has no use for "the common people," only as slaves to do her bidding. Then why should you grovel at her feet? Wealth is no part of man-hood, and manhood is the easiest thing in the universe to possess.

The politician will call upon you at your humble home, and you will throw open wide the doors of your hospitality, and he will endeavor to make you be-lieve that he considers you his equal.

Why does he do this?

Only to get your vote. Then you drop out of his mind until your services are again needed.

If you desire to test his sincerity call upon him

at his mansion, which he has been able to build from the honest sweat of your brow, and you will not find the same "politician" that you entertained with the lavish hand of good fellowship.

Oh! No! He has grown cold. Why thus? Simply because he is ashamed of you, and ashamed to be caught in your company, for fear some of his wealthy associates might see him.

Will he invite you to his home to spend the night with him as you did? NEVER.

Reader, this chapter is somewhat foreign to my idea relative to this book. However, "fashionable society" is so closely allied with "politics" that I could not fairly represent one without the other.

Was there ever a President of the United States elected without the "common people" did it? NEVER. Was there ever any man elected to public office without the "common people" were responsible for it? NEVER.

Do you know that the "common people" have it within their power to make men and undo them at their will? Then why should you "whimper" in the presence of wealth and permit "Fashionable Society" to cast her sneering remarks at you without making her feel the weight of your offended hand?

When you brand "Fashionable Society" as the "incubator of vice," and treat the politician who "truckles" to her infamous ways as a thing to be dreaded and a mortal to be despised, then you will purify the morals of our law-makers; as they are the "ringleaders" of this gang of degenerates who spend the money of the "common people" with the reckless hand of the profligate.

Give society to understand that you are acquainted with her unholy ways, and she will be compelled to respect you.

Teach your wives and daughters that to mingle with filthy "Fashionable society" is to lower themselves in the eyes of decency, and train your boys to turn a cold shoulder to the man who "truckles" to society's mandates, and you will mount at one bound to the pinnacle of greatness, and wealth will bow in humble submission to those to whom she should pay respectful homage, and to whom she must look for her existence, as the "common people," which "Fashionable society" brands as "the lower class," are the "bone and sinew," "brain and brawn" of this or any other land.

THE MOUNTAIN HOME OF LUCY STALEY, who was betrayed by one of Fashion's hyenas in men's clothes.

Chapter X.

The Sad History of Lucy Staley, a Beautiful Country Girl from the State of Colorado, Who Married a Disreputable Son of Wealth.

When a mother or father looks for the last time upon the beautiful face of their darling daughter who has been called from earth just as the tender bud of her girlhood is bursting into the beautiful flower of womanly beauty, it is sad indeed. However, they have a blessed consolation of knowing that while their poor hearts are bursting with grief the melody of heaven is sweeter by having added to that great angelic choir the voice of their precious child.

"Hope springs eternally in the bosom of man," and without it the human heart would be, indeed, a most wretched and desolate stretch of desert land.

DEATH! Oh, what a terrible thought to that mind which has never drank deep from the eternal spring of repentance, which bubbles close by the broad river of forgiveness.

DEATH! Oh, what a beautiful word to that tired soul which has been tossed to and fro upon the restless crest of earth's billowy deep, but tenaciously clung to "the promises of God," for well it knows that ere long life's tide will flow towards the glittering shores of peace, and land it in the realms of bliss, where earth's "shams" are forgotten and Heaven's beauties are everlasting.

Had Mr. and Mrs. Staley, father and mother of beautiful Lucy, their only child, have known she was to be sacrificed to the rapacious and damnable lust of Ralph Wyman, of New York, they would ten thousand times rather have followed her to her grave in that little country church yard upon the side of that towering Colorado mountain.

Lucy Staley was the only daughter of a loving and tender father and mother, who lived in the mountainous regions of Colorado, near a very fashionable health resort. Lucy's childhood had been spent in the quiet of this mountain neighborhood. Her avocation was that of helping her mother with the daily household duties, and assisting her father in taking care of his herd of Angora goats, as her father made his living by raising goats and honey, for he also had over one hundred hives of bees.

The reader can hardly think of a more picturesque home than that of Lucy Staley's, surrounded as it was by the hundred or more white houses of the busy bee and upward of five hundred goats, with their snowy fleeces. Of course, as could be expected, Lucy Staley was a petted child, but not a spoiled one by any means, as she had never been known to disobey a command of her father and mother, who were growing old, for they had never had a child to bless them until twenty years had rolled by after their marriage, and then this little, bright-eyed, sunny-haired mountain nymph made her appearance like a fairy to bless the declining years of their lives.

We have endeavored to give a picture of the home of Lucy Staley, so the reader might have an idea of what it was. However, the brush of the artist could not do justice to the subject. Therefore, we will try as near as possible to give you a pen picture of its beautiful simplicity.

The house was built of hewn logs, tastefully "chinked and daubed," and then whitewashed until it resembled a snow drift clinging to the side of the mountain slope.

In the rear of the little log cottage were the bee hives, scattered in artistic confusion, and at all times hundreds of goats could be seen with their young scampering over the cliffs that surrounded the cottage of this mountain beauty, as Lucy Staley was indeed a handsome girl.

The front of the house was covered with clinging vines that grew in profusion in this section of country, and the yard was a cluster of variegated mountain flowers.

The road wound from the valley below in a serpentine fashion, and many, many are the times that Lucy has traversed this rustic path with her father down to the little town that lay a mile and a half below heir cottage, and which is noted for its medicinal waters.

When Lucy would visit this mountain hamlet during the summer season, when the wealthy from all over the country were there, she would stand in childish amazement at the splendor of their dress. However, there was no spirit of restlessness or discontent within her bosom, as she loved her home and her parents with a true and tender love of a child of nature that she was.

Lucy grew from babyhood to childhood, and from childhood into girlhood, and from girlhood the blushing petals of womanhood unfolded in all their splendor of pure ladyhood, and still Lucy Staley loved her mountain home with a more tender effection.

Lucy, as might be expected, was the belle of this mountainous neighborhood, and she had a disposition that was the envy of all who knew her. The dark shadows that so often becloud the face of humanity never dared plant their ugly imprint upon the happy, sunlit countenance of Lucy.

Wherever there was trouble and misery among the inhabitants of this rural neighborhood, there the sweet smile, tender touch and cheery words of Lucy Staley were found.

Is it any wonder that this sunbeam of the mountain slope should be loved and respected by all who knew her?

Lucy's father and mother were honest, upright and honorable folks, as are the majority of such people who live to themselves, and who are permitted to

enjoy nature as she comes direct from the hand of
God. However, Lucy's parents were uneducated,
but Lucy had obtained a public school education,
and was thus enabled to read and write fairly well.
However, she was not versed in what society would
call accomplishments, but nevertheless Lucy Staley
possessed one accomplishment that made her as pure
as the mountain brook that bubbled forth from the
crest of the mountain that towered above her rustic
cottage, and that accomplishment was "untarnished
purity and womanhood."

It is strange, indeed, to know how one's life may
be completely changed by the most trivial occur-
rence, and such is the case in the life of Lucy Staley.

One bright, balmy morning in the latter part of
June Lucy was out upon the brow of the mountain
"rounding up" her father's goats in order to drive
them into the "goat lot," as the season for "shear-
ing" them was at hand.

Little did Lucy imagine that morning as she left
her vineclad home that before she reached it again
the Devil would ensnare her.

While Lucy Staley was coaxing the meek-faced
mother goats with their young down the mountain
slope, she heard the report of a gun near her, which

was no unusual thing, but immediately afterwards she heard the cry of some one in distress, and with a heart full of pity Lucy bounded from cliff to cliff until she reached the scene of misery, and there before her, stretched upon the grass, lay a young man, dressed in the fashion of a "city gentleman," with blood flowing from his left foot.

Ah! it would have been better for Lucy Staley to have steeled her heart and banished every tender feeling of mercy and humanity from that heart than for her to have answered the cry for help, as it cost her years of bitter repentance and days of bitter tears.

She reached the side of this "city gentleman," who was by name Ralph Wyman, the son of a multi-millionaire, from the great City of New York.

Lucy took in the surroundings at a glance, and hastily removed the shoe and stocking from Ralph Wyman's wounded foot, and then tore into strips her white apron and bound up the lacerated foot of this young man, which had received the accidental discharge of his gun while penetrating the underbrush of the mountain slope. Lucy stopped the flow of blood, and hurriedly gathered leaves to make a pillow for the head of this young man to rest upon, then disappeared like the flit of a sunbeam down the mountain slope to get help to bear Ralph Wyman to her home. In a few moments Lucy and her father gently lifted this wounded young man in their arms and bore him to their home to care for him. They learned that he was stopping in the valley at the hotel for his health, but, to their utter surprise, he begged them not to inform the landlord that he was injured, stating that, if they would consent, he would much prefer to remain at their home until his recovery, further stating that he would pay them the handsome amount of $25.00 per week as long as he stayed. This amount of money was a fortune in the eyes of this humble family, and they readily gave their consent, not so much, however, in order to obtain the money as it was the desire to grant the request of one in distress.

Ralph Wyman wrote a note to the landlord of the hotel, sending him what was due him for the time he had been stopping at the hotel, and informed him he would not return for some time, and old Mr. Staley that evening carried the letter down to the little town in the valley.

By the tender care of Lucy and her mother, Ralph Wyman was soon able to be out by the use of a crude crutch, made by Lucy's father, as the wound was but slight to begin with.

Up to the time that Ralph Wyman came upon the horizon of Lucy's life she had never had Cupid's dart to penetrate her heart, in fact, she had never encouraged any of the young men of that section who dared to make love to her; therefore Lucy was not versed in the arts of "Fashionable society," of which Ralph Wyman was considered a master. Consequently it was a very easy matter for this demon of society, which he proved himself to be, to ensnare innocent Lucy Staley into believing that he loved her with all his heart; as he unceasingly made love to her, not, however, for the purpose of making her his wife, but for the awful purpose of taking advantage of her childish confidence.

Oh! what a wretch, after receiving the treatment that he had at the hands of this family, and then to dare spread his infamous net of immorality about the pure form of this mountain nymph.

Had he forgotten Lucy's tender care during his afflictions? Had he forgotten those big brown eyes that swam in tears when she beheld him stretched upon the mountain side and could not help himself? Had he forgotten her father, bent with years, and this girl with their own hands gently carrying him down to their mountain home? Ah! No, he had not forgotten, but he lacked the noble principles of manhood; therefore he could not comprehend the obligations that he was under to this family, as no man who has been brought up in the atmosphere of "society abominations" can grasp the true meaning of true manhood.

Ralph Wyman unceasingly poured into Lucy's ears the torrent of his passions, clothed in language of love, which led this poor girl to believe that he sincerely and honestly loved her, as he had intimated time after time that his greatest desire was to make her his wife, but as soon as he found that Lucy was learning to love him with all her heart, he then began to scheme and plan for her destruction, but, be it said to the everlasting credit of this simple girl of the mountains, that she had been taught the lessons of virtue, and this scheming villain could not wrench from her the most precious jewel that belongs to womanhood.

Ralph Wyman was not a man to stop at anything, and he was determined to accomplish his dastardly purpose, regardless of consequences; therefore he proposed to Lucy that they be married at once, but

bound her under a solemn promise that she was not
to let his folks in the East know of their marriage for
a period of two years, telling her that a rich relative
of his had died and left him a large fortune, but one
of the provisions of the will was that if he married
within two years he was not to receive a cent, and
his portion was to go to his elder brother.

He never intimated the real reason why he did
not want his family, and especially his haughty and
ungodly mother, to know that he had married this
girl of the mountains, for if he had, he could never
have accomplished his purpose, as Lucy Staley would
never have entered into such an agreement with him,
for she would have discerned the reason that he
exacted this promise, which would have made her despise Ralph Wyman with the hatred only born in the
bosom of virtuous woman.

They were married by an old, retired country
minister, and lived at the home of Lucy's parents
until about the middle of September, when, as you
know, the majority of "city folks" return from the
country to their city homes. Lucy Staley loved her
husband with a pure love of a devoted wife, and she
in return received naught but the unholy and un-
sanctified passions of the brute she married.

As previously stated, about the middle of September Ralph Wyman informed his girl wife that he was compelled to go to the City of New York for a short time, to wind up his business, telling her that he would be back within a fortnight.

Lucy, loving, confiding, trusting wife, believed this "imp of Hell," and covered his unholy face with kisses that burned with the love of wifely devotion at his departure. He had promised to write to her as soon as he had arrived in New York, but ten days had glided by and no letter had come from her husband. However, Lucy had written every day since he had departed. Two weeks had passed and no tidings; three weeks had passed, and no tidings; four weeks had passed into history and no word from Ralph Wyman.

The first month had gone by and not a word, and Lucy, poor girl, still loved him with a devotion of an honest wife, and never dreamed that she had been betrayed and deserted.

The end of the second month came and passed, and not one word from her husband had she received, and each day Lucy or her poor old father would trudge to the postoffice and inquire for mail and each day she would mail a letter burdened with wifely love to that bundle of perfidy, whom she loved and admired better than she loved her own soul.

Month after month rolled by, and still no tidings from her degenerate husband came.

The dreary months of winter, with their snow and ice, had reluctantly yielded to the gentle touch of spring, but still no news had Lucy received from the man who had sworn to love and protect her.

April, with her showers and sunshine, had come again. May, with her wealth of blossoms, had dressed the mountain slopes in just as gorgeous fashion as before, but still poor Lucy Wyman could not be comforted.

On the second day of June Lucy Wyman became the mother of Ralph Wyman's child, which was a counterpart of its mother, for this little babe resembled her mother to such an extent that it was almost like her own picture in childhood.

Lucy resolved that she would go to the City of New York and find her husband, as she sincerely believed that when she presented herself to him with their sweet-faced babe she could woo him back again to her bosom.

Lucy's poor old father and mother tried to persuade her not to go, and succeeded for quite a while in their entreaties, but when autumn again returned and the yellow leaves began to carpet the earth with the dead hopes of summer, poor Lucy became melancholy and longed for her husband she loved so dearly, but who had betrayed her so shamefully.

Lucy's desire to go to New York to find her husband became so great that her father and mother at last gave their consent.

On the 15th of November Lucy and her baby departed from their mountain home to visit the great metropolis of the East. She arrived in that strange city of sights, and proceeded to locate the Wyman mansion, which was situated in the ultra-fashionable part of New York. With her babe to her bosom, she boldly marched to the front door of this grand mansion, and rang the door bell for admission.

The butler opened the door and inquired what she wanted, and stated that "beggars" should apply for help at the back door.

Lucy Wyman's cheeks burned with righteous indignation and informed this "brass-buttoned flunky" that she was no beggar and had not called for alms, but insisted that she be taken to see her husband. Ralph Wyman.

This "flunky" told her she was crazy and to be gone, but Lucy, with the determination of despair, stood her ground, and informed him she would stay there till the judgment day unless she was permitted to see her husband. He closed the door, and in a few moments a middle-aged lady appeared with a face hard as chiseled adamant and demanded an explanation of Lucy.

Lucy told her story of Ralph Wyman's courtship and marriage, and wound up by removing the veil from the face of her sleeping and beautiful babe, and held it out to her and exclaimed:" This is your legitimate grandchild, and your son, Ralph Wyman, is its father and my husband before God and under the laws of the State of Colorado," and with a sweep of her trembling hand she drew forth from her bosom her marriage certificate in evidence of the truthfulness of her statement.

The mother of Ralph Wyman was one of these cold, haughty, overbearing devotees of "Fashionable Society," who considered money above every other consideration known to man, and in order to get rid of Lucy invited her into the hall, and, with the brazenness of great wealth, informed Lucy she would give her ten thousand dollars to return to her Colo-

rado home, with the understanding that she bind herself in writing that she would never claim Ralph
Wyman again as her husband. She further stated
that unless she accepted this amount and complied
with her request, she would within thirty minutes
have her arrested, and both she and her bastard baby
would be thrown into jail, and it would be proven
that she was a lunatic.

Lucy Wyman's eyes glistened with the fire of
righteous indignation and with a voice as calm and as
subdued as the zephyr breeze that follows the furious storm exclaimed: "Do you presume to buy my
virtue and good name with your wealth, that perhaps carries with it the dark stains of human oppression? Do you expect me to raise this child of my
own blood and flesh and bring it up under a cloud
of its mother's virtue? NEVER! You can throw
me into jail if you like, and have a jury of your own
kind pass upon my sanity and prove me a lunatic, if
you please, but you will never buy my honor and good
name and blight the prospects of my innocent babe
with your wealth."

Lucy Wyman refused to leave this mansion,
which covered the unholy heads of the Wyman family, and was ruthlessly taken from the house by a

stalwart policeman, who was hired to do the bidding of society followers. After Lucy was taken from the Wyman mansion and led down the street by this blue-coated devil, who has no more regard for law and justice than Satan has for a saint, he informed Lucy if she would go about her business and not bother the Wyman's any more he would turn her loose, but unless she did, he would lock her up. and she would be considered a vagrant or crazy.

Lucy Wyman gave this policeman to understand that if she was released upon the streets of the great City of New York she would return to the Wyman residence, and there stand in front of the door of that mansion until the bleak winds of November froze both her and her baby into a frigid monument of Ralph Wyman's perfidy.

She was locked up by instructions of Ralph Wyman and his ungodly mother. She was forced to remain in this dungeon for twenty-two days. when her poor old father, learning of her misery, came to the city of New York and returned with her to her humble cottage upon the side of that mountain in the State of Colorado.

Lucy's friends knew that she was lawfully married to this wretch of society; therefore they consid-

(15)

ered her just as pure as they did before she was bound
by the laws of Colorado to this fiend, as wife. However, her life was blotted, and ever after that she
was not the same sweet-faced child of nature that
she had been before this dragon, which society calls
a "good fellow," entered her life, and endeavored to
rob her of her virtue without the binding obligation
of matrimony, but seeing that he could not accomplish his dastardly deed, he willingly took upon himself the solemn obligation of husband to break it
with as much unconcern as though the obligation
was taken for that purpose.

Lucy Wyman still lives in her mountain home, and
her baby girl, as she calls her, has grown into pure
womanhood, and joyously clambers from cliff to cliff
and skips down the same mountain paths that Lucy
once did, without the knowledge of the degeneracy
of her father.

Thus another blossom of virtue is plucked to have
its petals ruthlessly torn from its stem, to be trodden
upon by the ungodly feet of "society's demons."

A SOCIETY BALL: A common scene in fashionable society, where modesty is unknown.

Chapter XI.

A Page from the History of our Fore-fathers, Compared with our Present Surroundings.

Time has wrought many miraculous changes, and recorded many brave deeds of valor. She has plundered the minds of genius, and brought forth her mighty products. She has penetrated the bowels of the earth and uncovered her wealth which has been hidden from the eye of man for centuries.

Time has done many mighty wonderful things, but she has utterly failed to improve upon the character of our forefathers.

How did we find the morals of "society" when that old "Liberty Bell" pealed forth "INDEPENDENCE" to the inhabitants of this land?

How did we find the morals of "society" when George Washington's army of patriots left its imprint of blood upon the frozen ground at Valley Forge?

How did we find the morals of "society" when General Putnam left his plow and plunged into the battle field in defense of his country?

How did we find the morals of "society" when Ethan Allen demanded the British to surrender in the name of "The Great Jehovah, and the Continental Congress?"

Go read the records of our country's great, and learn the lesson that our forefathers taught, and you will find that the "Fashionable Society" of today, and the "Society" which our forefathers founded, are no more alike than the pomegranite, with her rich perfume, is like the thistle with its poisonous needles.

Who would dare question the acts of this grand army of patriots who endeared themselves to their country and painted with the brush of patriotism, their names in letters of fire, upon the walls of eternal greatness?

The man does not live who would dare besmirch the glorious name of one of them.

Look about for a moment, yea take years, and inquire of those we today call great, and learn if any one can be found who will tell you that the same spirit of manhood and patriotism permeates the nation's leaders, as when such women as "Molly Pitcher" were wives and mothers?

I did not say NONE, as it is the remnant that will furnish the salt, to save the earth.

Our land is dotted with educational institutions, and the clang of the school bell is heard upon every hand, and while the majority of our educators are men and women of pure clean characters they have that great and greedy host of wealth to combat with.

No man ever knew "Fashionable Society" except where great wealth abounds, and this same "Fashionable Society" endeavors to cover up her filthy trail by large donations to institutions of learning and charity. Wealth will rule with a hand of iron until her tyrannical tread becomes unbearable, and the "common people" register their protest, then some "pie-faced" follower of this "Society tribe," hired to do the bidding of wealth, will proclaim the "great and noble deeds" of John D. Rockefeller, or some other multi-millionaire. They will recount the great donations these men have made to institutions of learning and charity, and in a thousand other ways will endeavor to throw dust in the eyes of the "common people" in order to quiet them, for well they know should the "common people" become aroused to such an extent as to arise in one great body, they would shake the very foundations of the universe.

What would you think of a law that would permit your neighbor to rob you, and then escape punishment by returning just a part of his ill gotten gains?

The laws of our land are dictated by wealth. They are passed by the millionaire and his henchmen hired to do his bidding. Now do not understand me to say that all of our public servants are of this class, as it is not so, for we have some pure, noble minded officials, but the aim of wealth and "Fashionable Society" which are one and the same, is to be represented in the law making bodies of our land, and until the "common people" take a stand against it, and stop "throwing up their hats" and screaming their fool selves hoarse over some donation made by wealth, which is only a small part they were robbed of, they will always be slaves to this gang of pirates.

It will take a keen eye and a clear brain to discern between the rulers of this country and that of

Monarchial Governments. The greatest difference that you will discern is, that this country is ruled by men of wealth elected by the "common people," and Monarchial countries are ruled by despots who claim to rule by "Divine right," either of which is a disgrace to mankind. Both classes are disreputable to a greater or less degree, and have no interest in those they rule, only as far as they can be used to their own advantage, which means servitude and misery to the ones governed.

It might seem to the reader that "Fashionable Society" and the contents of this chapter were foreign to each other. However they are one and the same, as Washington, D. C., is the incubator of wealth, and wealth is the parent of "Fashionable Society," and either would famish and become a thing of the past without the other.

Reader, do not get "Fashionable Society" and "Polite Society" confused, as the two are no more alike than the darkness of the caverns of the earth are like the effulgency of the noonday sun.

"Polite Society" is composed of brains and manhood. Of honesty and integrity. Of kindness towards their fellowman. Of purity of mind. Of virtue and womanhood, and above all JUSTICE.

"Fashionable Society" as we see it at the ballroom of fashion, and reclining in the mansions of the millionaire, and parading in the public places of our large cities, is everything that "Polite Society" is not.

"Fashionable Society" is haughty. She is brazen and at all times endeavors to parade her wealth, which could not be a better indication of her vulgarity. She looks with contempt upon those who do not possess wealth, which proves that she is void of principle. She dresses herself in the garb of immodesty and immorality, which is indicative of her depravity. She "WALKS IN THE WAYS OF THE UNGODLY, AND SITS IN THE SEAT OF THE SCORNFUL," which proves her to be unclean. In fact she becomes abhorrent by her disrespect for the laws of God and man, and a thing to be despised and dreaded as the vilest reptile.

Our forefathers never dreamed that their glorious works of patriotism would be marred by the greedy and unholy hand of wealth. They looked out upon the broad expanse of the "new world," and beheld a land rich with the gifts of God. A land which would furnish an abiding place for the oppressed nations of the earth. They never dreamed that within a short period of a century and a quarter after the Declaration of Independence was declared, that wealth would march through the land with the arrogance of the tyrannical despot they left behind.

Ah! it is a sickening sight to see, this proud old land, "The home of the brave and the land of the free" bowing to titled royalty and sending a representative across the waters to pay homage to King Edward the VII. of England. Me thinks I hear Washington exclaim "Shame! shame!" I hear Patrick Henry's "GIVE ME LIBERTY OR GIVE ME DEATH," ringing in my ears. In my imagination I see the rugged form of General Putnam stalking through the land in mighty wrath. Me thinks I hear Ethan Allen exclaim, "This is not the America of 1776."

In my mind's eye I see upon the battlements of heaven Gen. Robert E. Lee scanning the horizon with pallid cheek, and exclaim to his comrades in gray: "We lost the fight for what we thought was right, but the defeat was nothing, compared to the defeat patriotism has suffered by being dragged across the ocean and forced to bow at royalty's feet."

I see in my imagination, Gen. Grant shading his eyes and looking out from the walls of "The New Jerusalem," and in thunderous tones exclaim "Who dared to pull down the flag of our beloved land, and trail it in the slime of Nobility?"

"Like begets like," and wealth craves for the gaudy apparel of kings and queens, therefore America with the fashionable "Hag" of society upon one hand, and her twin sister wealth, upon the other, has for the first time in history, lowered the bright colors of Liberty and Patriotism, while the wealthy "idiots" of this country kiss the hand of England's profligate King.

The difference in the character of our forefathers and that of our leaders of today, is simply this. One looked to God for wisdom to guide their actions, and the other depends solely upon the power of their wealth, and whenever a Nation loses sight of her Creator, honor and manhood decays, and virtue is trampled under foot by the maddening throng of depraved men.

Whenever the "common people" wake up to the fact that the unholy chase for wealth is the cause of the majority of our National evils, then and not until then, will the white winged dove of contentment hover about us. Just as soon as we realize that the "common people" are good enough to fill the offices which are the gift of the "common people," then we will drive drunkenness and harlotism from the places where honor and virtue should dwell, and teach wealth that HONOR is the password to "polite society."

When that time comes "Fashionable Society" will be relegated to the haunts of open sin, and not permitted to wrap about her ungodly form the mantle of honor which she so ruthlessly tramples under her degraded feet.

Woo back the spirit of our forefathers, and the form of questionable "society" will drag her filthy self from the seats of honor which she has so long disgraced.

SOCIETY AND ITS RESULTS—Ladies under the influence of Rum being led to their carriages.

Chapter XII.

Gambling Among "Fashionable Society."

To the uninitiated country man and woman, who have been brought up to look upon the sin of gambling as one of the most degrading things imaginable, they will hardly believe that members of "Fashionable Society" with scarcely an exception, are inveterate gamblers, but nevertheless such is the case.

What I will relate in this chapter is not what I have heard, but is what I have seen with my own eyes, and I frankly acknowledge that I had associated with this class of people for so long, that I was made to become one of this unholy class.

You will often hear "Society folks" talk about "Euchre parties," but you will never hear them acknowledge they gamble, and it is a known fact among those who have associated with this class of people, that they not only gamble for small amounts, but they will wager large amounts, and the only difference between the "Fashionable Gambling" houses and what you would call a "Gambling Den" is, that these "Gambling Dens" are subject to raid by the officers of the law, for they make no pretense of being anything but gambling houses.

However, upon the other hand, "Fashionable Society" does not have as much respect for their individual homes as the vilest kind of a gambler, for this "Fashionable" herd will open up a game of chance right in their own parlors, which renders them almost immune from arrest, by the police officer that travels their beat, for two reasons. First, the policeman does not know that gambling is being carried on in this elegant mansion in the fashionable part of a city, and the second reason why their houses are not raided the same as that of common gamblers is, because should such a move be put on foot, they will hush it up with their millions.

I remember distinctly the first time I ever saw a game of what is called "Draw Poker" played in my life, as in my boyhood days my dear old father and

mother taught me to believe that card playing was
not right, and that gambling was the most degrading
thing that a young man could get in the habit of doing, therefore, when my fortune was left me by my
old aunt, I was ignorant of any game of cards, in fact
I did not know one card from the other.

Soon after reaching the City of Washington, I
was invited by one of my gentleman (?) friends, to call
at his house, as he stated they were going to have
a little game of cards for amusement.

I told him I knew nothing about cards, for I had
never played a game of cards in my life, and he
seemed to be very much astonished at my "ignorance."
You may call it "ignorance" if you like, but I would
consider it a great compliment to have the world
know that I had never seen a game of cards played.
However such can not be the case, as my first lessons
in such matters were unheeded, but thank God my
"second sight," as it were, has returned to me and the
teachings of my youth looms up before me with wonderful power.

I called upon this young gentleman (?) after supper, and about ten o'clock an ivory topped table was
wheeled to the center of the room and the other guests
were invited to "set around."

There were others there besides myself, not only gentlemen but ladies, and when the ladies deliberately took their places around this ivory topped "Implement of Hell" called by "Society" a "Poker Table" I was indeed astonished, as I had only gotten an introduction to these ladies that evening, therefore I was surprised to know how familiar they could become on such short notice, but my greatest wonderment seized me when my young gentleman friend wanted to know what the "limit" would be. I knew nothing about what "Poker" was, neither did I know what "limit" meant, only I imagined there must be an element of chance attached to its meaning, but I at that time considered it would be a disgrace to let this elegant (?) "Society" know that I was a "Tenderfoot" in the ways of the Devil, so I pushed up my chair like an "old timer," of course not thinking for a moment that I was to be robbed by my friends in their own homes.

I resolved that there was no better time in the world for me to learn how to play "Poker" than at that time, so I kept a keen lookout for a few moments until I got the run of the game, at the same time I was bewildered by the expressions of "ante," "limit," "Jackpot" and such other language as is used among the gambling fraternity, but within half an hour I had been made familiar with what these names meant. My female associates manipulated the cards and used the language of the game with as much ease as the commonest kind of a "Nigger" would, playing this game on a box in a back alley.

I, of course, had but very little money with me, perhaps a couple of hundred dollars, but I never dreamed that I had been invited to this elegant mansion, which was the home of "Fashionable Society" to participate in a game where the predominating spirit was MONEY, as I believed when I received the invitation that it was to be a social game of cards for pastime, never dreaming there was to be a money consideration.

After the game had started and I learned they were playing for money, the thought struck me that it would be for only a small amount, and just enough to "make the game interesting" as the "Society lady" calls it, but before we had gone far, I realized the fact that these elegant gentlemen (?) and those perfumed ladies (?) were out for no other purpose than to make money. I wanted to play the part of a "dead game sport" as I did not have sense enough and manhood enough about me to tell them that I considered playing for money in the mansions of the wealthy as disreputable as "Shooting Craps" with a common "coon."

At first I won a little money, but after a while I began to have to visit my pocket-book very frequently, and before eleven o'clock it was empty, and I was short something like One Hundred and Seventy-five or Two Hundred Dollars. I had my check book in my pocket, and I asked them if any one would cash my check for Five Hundred Dollars, which accommodation I soon received.

Within a short time my elegant "Society" friends played for big stakes and before I left that gambling den, about four o'clock in the morning, I had not only spent the One Hundred and Seventy-five or Two Hundred Dollars in cash that I brought with me, but ι had issued my checks for over Seven Thousand Dollars.

Where had it gone, and who had received this money?

Oh, no one but my elegant friends (?) who had invited me to their home and robbed me with as little compunction of conscience as the highwayman with masked face would take your money from you at the point of his revolver.

I had learned to play "Poker" and paid well for my first lesson.

Had I have had as much sense as a "load of old shoes" I, right then and there, would have turned my back on "Fashionable Society," but the glitter of gold and the flash of their diamonds had so bewildered me that I was almost as helpless to leave these "Palaces of Sin" as the poor moth is, to pull herself away from the bright blaze of the candle.

To my certain knowledge Miss Etta Bartley, who was the Niece of a Senator, received over Two Thousand Dollars of my poor old Aunt's money, and if any one would have called Miss Etta Bartley a gambler, she would have died with heart disease in four minutes.

I never knew for a certainty, but I will always believe that that game of "Poker" was a set up job on me, and that I was deliberately robbed of my money, however, I could not prove this to be true, but I know one thing, and that is this, that I got exactly what was due me, and I have no sympathy for any man who has not manhood and sense enough to refuse to drink poison, when he knows that it is poison.

I have had several invitations to play "Poker" since that night, and have accepted one or two invitations, but never lost any great amount of money, as I soon learned that these "Society" people played

"Poker" for what there was in it, in fact, they make it a business and at least one-fourth of these butterflies of fashion, who parade as "pure women," obtain their finery by the degrading practice of gambling.

You may not know it, but the majority of our Congressmen and Senators whom we send to Washington City play "Poker," and other games of chance, and they do not play them for pastime, but they actually play for money, but they would tell you they only played for "fun."

No man or woman that lives can indulge in an evil "for fun" and make a practice of this evil and not leave the taint of sin upon them, as it would be just as impossible to empty a cup of filthy water into a bucket of pure spring water, and leave it as clear afterwards as before, as it would be to follow the ways of the sinner and not become sinful.

We find gambling among our Church members, as they will give these "Euchre Parties," which are the Devil's own institution, and will charge each one who participates in the game a fee of 25 or 50 cents and will give a prize to the one who wins the most games.

This money they collect as a "fee" for playing the games, goes to the Church. Think of it, money ob-

tained in this manner being donated and used by a
Church which holds Christ and Him crucified up to
the sinner as an example, when the members will resort to such ungodly methods to obtain money; and
the preacher, be it said to his everlasting disgrace,
often smiles upon such actions.

The trouble with the American people and in fact
all other nations is, that they endeavor to "mimic"
the actions of the wealthy, and you will find the "common people" giving "Euchre Parties" for the benefit
of the Church, simply because they want to impress
their neighbors that they are "up-to-date" and doing
what "Fashionable Society" does, and just as long
as the "common people" try to follow the footsteps of
"Fashionable Society" just that long humanity will
be degraded, for any man or woman who will try to
keep pace with this "renegade tribe of the Devil's
own" just that long sin, vice, and immorality will remain to curse us.

Be it said to the everlasting credit of those who
live in the country and in smaller towns, they do not
practice the abominations found in larger cities, and
the man or woman who would endeavor to introduce
these scandalous practices in the country would be
treated as a person to be dreaded, and abhorred and

dangerous to the morals of any neighborhood. Such would be a righteous judgment, for you can not set the proper example before the young and follow exactly the same practices and customs as the young knows the sinner to follow.

"Fashionable Society" always plays the part of morality, decency and christianity, as they have long since learned that in order to more easily lead the "common people" in their trail of debauchery, they must play the part of "saint."

If it is wrong for the keeper of a "bar-room" to have gambling in his establishment, it is wrong for "society" to gamble in her mansions. If it is wrong for the poor man to drink wine from the counter of the "common saloon" it is an abomination for the wealthy to drink it from their ivory topped tables. If it is a sin for the laboring man to obtain the money of his associates by the degrading practice of gambling, it is a sin for the diamond bedecked hand of wealth to take the money in the same manner from her associates.

There is no sin that will contaminate and sink into perdition the soul of the poor man, that will not eternally damn the soul of the rich.

I have visited homes where extravagant elegance

was visible upon every hand, and where they presumed to set the example of fashion, of morals and of politeness to the "common people," when if the laboring man, the mechanic or the merchant would endeavor to follow their example, he would not only wreck his business and wreck his character, but would eternally damn his soul and would be looked upon as a character that no decent man or woman could afford to pattern after.

I remember being in Philadelphia, visiting some of this "highly perfumed set" and received an invitation to a "card party" to be given at the home of one of "Society's followers" and of course like a "truckling fool" that I was, I went. However, by this time I had learned that "Card Parties" and "Euchre Parties" and anything that had "cards" attached to it, meant nine times out of ten that gambling would be the order of the day, but I am glad to say that I had been taught a lesson in cards that I had not forgotten; in fact gambling was one of society's sins that did not interest me a particle and the only reason that I was persuaded into it was on the account of trying to "look smart" and not having moral courage to say "NO."

My friends and I called that evening at the home

of our friends where the "card party" was to be given, and of course "elegant society" (?) was there in all of her grandeur, and the Devil also was there with his paraphernalia of Hell, his wine, champagne, cards and every other sin known to the vocabulary of the Devil.

After an hour of silly prattle by all of us, the presiding lady of that home gently pulled down the blinds of that splendid double parlor, which meant as I had long since learned, that a card game was about to open in "full blast." I think there was something like six or seven ladies and about as many gentlemen who sat around that Ivory Topped Table to play "Poker" like inveterate gamblers.

This class of people invariably commence by playing for a penny or not more than five cents, which is done in order to entice every one of the party to "take a hand" and this innocent looking pastime generally entices all of the party to "set up" to the table.

"Society" well knows if she can get one of her "dupes" started in the game that they would feel humiliated to drop out, which will enable the most scientific of the game to fleece the unsuspecting "Fashionable idiot."

"This card party" was near the farthest end of

my society career and I was not very particular whether they liked me or not, as I had about come to the
conclusion that the whole thing was an abomination
and a disgrace to mankind, therefore I had become
more outspoken in regard to my likes and dislikes
and I could say "NO" with considerable emphasis,
consequently when one of these sweet faced Devils
of "Society" with her bewitching smile says "Col. Maple, aren't you going to play with us?" I bluntly said
"No, as I had had my eye-teeth cut long since," which
seemed to considerably disturb the "painted countenance" of my "she beauty." However, I was not particular whether she liked it or not, and I took no part
in the game, but sat by as an interested spectator and
gazed upon the cunning and disreputable practices of
this "Society gang" in order to obtain money from
their associates.

It has always seemed to me that the women of
"Society" were better players than the men, or at
least, they always won more money than the male contingent, and I was unable to discern whether it was
actually because they were better players or better
thieves, and before that game was over I was pretty
well convinced that it was on the account of the ladies (?) being better thieves than the gentlemen, for

I sat around that "Ivory topped Table" and beheld
schemes and tricks that would have cost a professional gambler his life, had his villainy been detected
by his associates.

One of the ladies who was engaged in this game
was a Miss Orton from the State of Ohio, and who I
understood was quite wealthy.

This girl lost heavily that night and from her deep
concern in the game, and from the look of despair
when she would lose, would lead any one to believe
that her finances were at least getting towards the
point where the loss of money hurt, as she became
nervous and "rattled" and drank wine and champagne
with the recklessness of a toper, but you must bear
in mind, kind reader, that wine and champagne is a
bosom companion in all of these gambling socials
among the rich, for wine is used for a stimulant and
as the motive power which forces the "Moneyed fool"
to lose his cash for the benefit of the "wise ones,"
therefore it would be impossible to systematically rob
their companions without the use of alcoholic stimu-
lants.

Miss Orton had lost quite a little fortune, perhaps
Fifteen Hundred or Two Thousand Dollars, when she
burst into tears and stated that she did not have an-

other cent with her, and would not draw her check for
another dollar, as she was in "bad luck," but bantered
any man around the table to play her "One Hundred
Dollars against a kiss." Of course these "biped imps"
were forced to be gallant and the challenge was accepted, and a young man by the name of Earley accepted the proposition, and this poor girl lost again,
and brazenly before her companions paid the debt.

In my estimation she might as well have gambled
her virtue against the $100.00 as to have done what
she did, for it was a step in that direction, to say the
least of it.

If the devotees of "Fashionable Society" who claim
the right of setting the example for the masses, are
so corrupt as to resort to every deception known to
the lowest class of mankind, then pray tell me the difference between the two, with the exception, however,
of one class having money and the other not.

A man or woman who will sit around the table
with this tribe of fashion, and who plays in their
games can not detect their tricks and schemes they
resort to in order to win your money, but if you will
sit by as a spectator you can readily understand why
some are more "lucky" than others, as in fact there
is no such a thing as "luck" to the gambling frater-

nity or "Fashionable Society," as they will not trust
"fickle luck" for their success, but they resort to
tricks which are considered disreputable by wide open
"Gambling Dens" and any man who would practice
such trickery in one of them and it was found out upon him, he would either pay the penalty with his life,
or be the recipient of a huge thrashing.

This "Fashionable tribe" had to learn these tricks
from some one, as they do not present themselves to
any one in a beautiful nightly vision. Now if they
had to be taught these tricks called the "Gambler's
art" they had to gain their information from some
"Red handed" frequenter of "Gambling Dens" and if
"Society" will stoop so low as to practice upon her
associates the schemes and tricks that she learned
from the lowest characters on earth, then what right
has this "brazen jade" to claim the right to set the
example for humanity?

Whenever I hear of a "Euchre Party" or "Card
party," I wonder what the mothers and fathers of this
land can mean by permitting their pure girls and their
noble sons to attend them, for it is in the Parlors of
"Fashionable Society" and the ones who try to
"mimic" her, that the first principles for the mania
of gambling is founded, and where the first lessons of

Harlotism, vice and degradation is instilled in the minds of the young.

The sins of the drunkard in the gutter have no attraction for the young, as they consider them an abomination. The blear eyed countenance of the disreputable woman and her profane language have no attraction for the young. No sin that is committed by the lowest element of the universe attracts the attention and admiration of the young man and woman, but Ah! where the trouble lies is the sins committed by what the world calls the "Leaders of Society" with her gaudy apparel and rich equippage, for the young man and woman of this country try to imitate this class, they believing that it is the "proper thing" simply because wealth is permitted to go unrebuked.

I could mention, I suppose, fifty different experiences that I have had with this "Fashionable Gang" where the magnificent parlors of their mansions were turned into "Gambling Hells."

I would advise the fathers and mothers of this land to look with as much contempt upon the "Euchre Parties" and "Card Parties" given by their neighbors and by the Church members, as they would upon the open "Gambling Dens" attached to the bar rooms, for these "Euchre Parties" and "Card Socials" are the

stepping stones that leads to the misery incidental to
the crime of Gambling. When sin and immorality
committed by the rich and "Fashionable Society" is
punished in the same manner, as when committed by
the poor wretch of God's universe, then the young
and rising generation will learn that sin and immorality is an abomination and the destroyer of character
regardless of whether it is committed by the pauper
in rags, or the millionaire in his "purple and fine
linen."

MODESTY, WHERE ART THOU?" A sight where modesty is not seen, and where virtue nears the abyss of shame.

Chapter XIII.

"Fashionable Summer Resorts."

In this chapter we will endeavor to give the reader a "stop over" at some of our so-called "Fashionable Summer Resorts," for a short stay.

Poor, or "common people" can not visit these places because everything is "so high" that none but the wealthy can afford such luxuries.

Did I say everything was "high?" Yes, I said it, but I meant "some things" only, as the standard of morality and manhood is not "high," or at least the scale would not be considered "high," if measured by the "Golden Rule."

In the first place we want to give you an introduction to the people you are compelled to "mix" with at these places, and you MUST "mix" with them if they

have money, as wealth, you know, is the only re-
quirement you must meet at these places.

I will now introduce you to Mrs. Brewer, who is
the wife of Mr. Hop Brewer, who is the millionaire
distiller of St. Louis, or some other place, and who
has made his millions by furnishing transportation
to Hell for thousands, yea tens of thousands of his
fellowmen.

Mrs. Brewer is a florid looking creature, that prob-
ably would not weigh a ton, as she has not been able
to drink the entire output of her husband's distillery.
We also want you to meet her "sweet scented" husband, Mr. Hop Brewer. This is he, I guess you would
have known him any where, as they all look alike.
See him strut around with his important air. See him
spend his wealth with lavish hand. Every dollar he
spends is wet with the tears of mothers, widows and
orphans whom he has robbed of their sons, husbands
and fathers, but what does "Fashionable Society"
care, just so long as he has money?

Oh, here is Mrs. Grainpit, and it would not do for
you to miss meeting her, as she is the wife of the
man who cleared $1,000,000.00 in one day on the
Board of Trade, by squeezing the very life out of his
neighbors, and bringing their families to want.

"Fashionable Society" falls at the feet of Mr. and Mrs. Grainpit, and why not? As they are wealthy, and whose business is it how they got their money?

"Fashionable Society" would "turn up" their "red noses" at a common every day saloon keeper, but they simply "eat up" the man who furnishes the product for these "common Saloon Keepers," to run their "Hell Holes" with.

"Fashionable Society" would be horrified to come into contact with the poor miserable mortal who had stolen a loaf of bread to feed his famishing family with, but they simply "slobber" all over the big thief who robbed his neighbors, by manipulating the market, and "Squeezing" the last dollar from them.

Oh! I beg your pardon, Mrs. Landlord, I did not know you were here. Mrs. Landlord is the wife of old "pious" John Landlord, who lives in elegant style in the most fashionable part of the city, and goes to his agent and rakes in his thousands each month for "rents" collected from the "brothels" and "Bar-rooms" which occupy his property.

Mr. Landlord is known as the "Retired Capitalist" who lives off of the income of his property. Both he and his wife belong to Rev. Takeall's church, which is considered the "swellest" church in the city.

Rev. Takeall don't care where the money comes from just so he gets it, and never asks any questions, but closes his ungodly eyes, and says, "The Lord loveth a cheerful giver."

Old Brother Landlord and his wife "pitch in" with lavish hand as the contribution box passes, and each dollar bears the imprint of immorality, shame, vice and debauchery, for his "rents" come from the occupants of houses of "ill-fame" and "Bar-rooms."

If you would introduce "Fashionable Society" to old Landlord's tenants, they would have eighty-three fits before you could throw water in their face, but they "bow down" and worship this old cur whose soul would rattle in the hull of a mustard seed, like "three dimes" in a sugar hogshead.

But what is it "Society's" business how this pious old hypocrite got his money, just so he has it?

But here is Mrs. Fasthorse and her husband. Bless their "tainted souls," I was about to forget them. This man, and his wife as well, make no "bones" of "gambling" on horseraces, in fact they have to gamble to live, as Mr. Fasthorse is a "horseman" and his dear wife is "Horsey" looking, whether she be a "horse-woman" or not.

This "perfumed pair" follow the races from city

to city and cause once honest young men to rob their employers in order to bet on the races. This is the "pair" that causes men to mortgage their little homes in order to "pick the winner," for they spend their money with lavish hand, therefore they must have money, no matter if humanity suffers.

Suppose that I take you around to the "Club House" of one of these "summer resorts" and let you peep in. What do you think you would find?

Well, you will find Mr. Brewer, the millionaire distiller, who furnishes his neighbors with transportation to Hell. You will find Mr. Grainpit, the man who made a "million" in one day by robbing his neighbors. You will find old "pious" John Landlord, who lives off the rents he collects from his tenants who run houses of "ill-fame" and "Barrooms." You will find Mr. Fasthorse, who causes the young men to rob their employers to raise money to gamble with.

What is this "Club House?" Oh! nothing but a "Saloon." Just the same as any other "doggery" with the exception of it being a "Palace of Sin," while the other one is only a common Bar-room for "common people."

Is that the only difference?

Yes, only you find big thieves there who have

stolen millions, while at the other saloons you only find a class of petit thieves, as they never had an opportunity to get big "swag."

What are they doing at this "Club House?" Oh, nothing only "drinking," just the same as any other "toper," only they have "cut glass" goblets, and sip it through a "straw," as they have plenty of time, while the "common people" are in a hurry and drink out of a tin cup, or any old thing.

"You don't say so?" Yes, I do, and if you will wait until about two o'clock in the morning you will see this "gang" "fumbling" along towards their room with a "load" that would break the back of a camel.

What have they been doing until two o'clock? Oh, nothing only gambling, and trying to rob one another. Do these "old fellows" who go off for the summer actually gamble? Why bless your poor ignorant souls, that is why they go, as they have had to remain "sorter" half way decent while at home, therefore they take their "outings" to get their "hides full" and do everything else that their depraved natures crave.

Now, Mr. Maple, do you actually think this is so? Oh, don't ask me such questions, as I am not "thinking" about this matter, for I have been "ALL ALONG THE LINE," and I KNOW.

Reader, I have given you an insight to the class of people that frequents these "Fashionable" resorts.

However, I have not told you that while these old reprobates were drinking and gambling until two o'clock each night, their "simpering" old wives were "huddled up" in some dark corner at the Hotel allowing some young "flirt" to make love to them, and their daughters were either following the example of their mothers or doing worse.

I have been to Atlantic City, and Coney Island, where "Fashionable Society" was upon every hand, and where wealth was counted by hundreds of millions, and I have seen sights among this class that were so disgusting that I would not dare put it in print.

What more could you expect from this class of people? You come in contact and "mix" with those who have money, and the majority of our great moneyed men came into possession of their millions by very questionable methods.

I have stood upon the beach at Atlantic City and seen hundreds of the daughters of wealth emerge from the bath houses with so little clothing upon their person that you would have to look twice to see whether they were mermaids or human beings.

The "swellest" suits at these sea shore summer resorts are those that take up the least room in one's trunk, and are the nearest the color of human flesh.

I say it, and I believe that any true woman who possesses the purity of womanhood will bear me out in the assertion, that no woman can unblushingly dress in such a garb without lowering herself, not only in the estimation of humanity, but she loses respect for herself.

I have seen young men and women go bathing together with scarcely any clothes upon their person, and they would become so familiar in their actions that the modest onlookers would actually turn their heads in disgust.

It is the "plump," well-formed girls of fashion who invariably possess the most abbreviated costume, as the "skinny" individual invariably plays the part of "modesty," for she has no plump limbs to exhibit, therefore her bathing costume resembles a full-grown "mackintosh."

If it is immoral for a lady to go half clad in the presence of gentlemen at home it is surely just as immodest and immoral to do the same thing away from home and in the presence of a multitude of strangers.

I remember seeing a sweet-facd young girl at Atlantic City in company with her mother, who seemed to be shocked at nearly everything she saw, and I knew that it was not "assumed modesty," as a womanly flush of shame would mantel her cheek when these "society girls" would brazenly perform some act of their many very questionable ones.

Her mother was visibly embarrassed by the open acts of immodesty by these devotees of fashion, and I could notice that this mother and daughter endeavored to keep to themselves as much as possible.

I resolved to make the acquaintance of this mother and daughter if possible, so I managed through a friend to get an introduction to them and learned that it was their first visit to "such a place," as the mother termed it.

I learned that a rich uncle had died and left the mother considerable money, and of course this mother thought she was bound to get her daughter into society, therefore concluded to make the "plunge" at Atlantic City.

They were from the State of Kentucky and had been used to good society. What I mean by "good society" is "polite society."

Mrs. Groves and her daughter, as Groves was their name, informed me that as soon as their month was up they intended to return home, for they stated they had paid a month's board and did not care to lose it.

I remarked to the mother, if she did not think it would be better to lose a month's board than to run the risk of having her darling daughter lose her modesty and her childish purity.

Mrs. Groves retorted that she was not afraid of that, stating "that Margaret had been too well raised to be led astray by "this class of coarse people" as she termed them.

Ah, how the words of poor Mrs. Frankness rang in my ears, as the reader will remember that Grace Frankness committed suicide to hide her shame and her mother had thought that her children's early lessons were proof against the snares of "Society."

I let the subject drop as I saw that Mrs. Groves had taken offense at what I said.

It was only a few days until I saw a young man by the name of Lathrop from Cincinnati, "gallanting" around with Margaret Groves. I did not know Lathrop, only his actions were evidence enough for me as to his character. I afterwards learned that his father was a wholesale liquor dealer in Cincinnati.

In a few evenings I saw young Lathrop and Margaret Groves out riding and I said to myself, "It won't be long until Miss Margaret will be going the "gaits."

In less than ten days from the time I had the first talk with Mrs. Groves and her daughter, I beheld Margaret Groves lying in the sand upon the beach with young Lathrop, dressed in a bathing costume that was as abbreviated as any to be seen.

To my surprise Mrs. Groves and her daughter quit speaking to me, in fact they would not recognize me when they met me.

I had done nothing to offend them, unless it was by stating to Mrs. Groves that perhaps it would be better to lose a month's board than to run the risk of her daughter losing her childish modesty.

Within a very short time Margaret Groves was going a gait that surely leads to destruction. I noticed that Mrs. Groves did not leave when her month was up, so I concluded that she had come to the conclusion that the people at Atlantic City were not so "shocking" as she first thought.

I kept a close watch on Margaret Groves, as I was desirous to know just what would be the outcome of her first summer among this herd of "Society Devils."

It was not long until I found young Lathrop and Margaret in the "green room" of a public place of amusement.

A green room, dear reader, is a place where "drinks" are served, and out of sight of the eye of decency.

I noticed that Margaret's cheeks were flushed and she talked in an unnatural manner which was all the evidence that I needed that Marget Groves was nearing the chasm of shame.

I turned from the scene with a heavy heart as I was convinced that young Lathrop meant her destruction.

The season was nearing the close when one morning I received a letter from Mrs. Groves requesting me to call at her suite of rooms at once. I surmised the nature of her request, but I hurriedly made my way up to Mrs. Groves' rooms and found her weeping as though her heart would break. I inquired the cause of her grief and she informed me that Margaret had not returned to her room the previous night, and stated that she was afraid something awful had befallen her.

She wound up by saying, "Oh! Colonel Maple, if I had only taken your warning and left this city of awful shames, my poor darling Margaret would not have been led astray and my poor old heart would not be breaking as it is."

I promised to do all for her I could and set out with a determination to find Margaret Groves, if possible.

I felt quite sure that young Lathrop, the villain, was with her, and surmised that they had gone to Philadelphia, as it is not far from Atlantic City, where one can so easily and quickly hide themselves from the world.

I told Mrs. Groves that I would do all I could, and she says: "Oh! Colonel, help me find my darling. and I will at once leave this awful, awful city of wickedness."

I could do nothing but wait developments, as I was quite sure they would return soon, but I carefully watched each train as it pulled in from Philadelphia, and that evening about 10 o'clock my watchfulness was rewarded by seeing Margaret Groves and her friend, young Lathrop, step off of one of the middle coaches.

I followed them nearly to their hotel, when Lathrop left her and Margaret proceeded alone.

Next morning I called on Mrs. Groves and inquired if she had heard anything from Margaret, as I did not tell her what I had seen, as I was quite sure that Margaret would tell a tale to suit herself.

Mrs. Groves informed me that she had judged poor Margaret wrongfully, as she and a number of other girls had gone to New York City on an excursion, and had told Mr. Lathrop to tell her.

In a short time young Lathrop put in his appearance and begged Mrs. Groves' pardon for not telling her, stating that he had been called out of the city suddenly, showing a telegram as evidence, and had forgotten it, and in very humble tones over and over begged Mrs. Groves' forgiveness.

This poor old confiding and ignorant mother believed their falsehood, and actually within a day or two again refused to speak to me.

The day I left Atlantic City I wrote a letter to Mrs. Groves telling her exactly what I had seen with my own eyes, as I thought it was my duty, and thought she should know it, so that she could, if possible, save her daughter from the sure fate of shame, and disgrace that awaited her.

It was nine years from that time, when I chanced to be going by train from Louisville, Ky., to Nashville, Tenn., when in front of me sat an old decrepit white haired lady who bore the deep lines of sorrow on her countenance. It seemed as though her face was familiar, however I could not remember where I had ever seen it.

When we were nearing Elizabthtown, Ky., this old lady endeavored to close the window of the coach, but could not do it. I performed the task for her, and when she turned to thank me, she almost gasped for breath and exclaimed: "Ain't this Colonel Maple?"

I informed her that it was, and she sobbed as though her heart would break and said: "My name is Groves, and my prayers have been answered, for I have prayed earnestly to God that he would permit me to see you before I died, as I wanted to thank you for the advice I would not take."

I inquired where Margaret was, and this poor old heart-broken mother replied: "In the mad house."

It was some time before she could compose herself sufficiently to talk, but when she did, she told me that their stay at Atlantic City was the beginning of Margaret's downfall, and stated that it seemed as though she endeavored to climb to the greatest height of frivolity, and then as suddenly turned "all holts loose" and plunged headlong to the very bottomless pit of shame.

She said that Margaret went from bad to worse, and that she had spent all she had in trying to reclaim her, and at last had to place her in a "mad house" for she had become a raving maniac. She also informed me when I left her at Gallatin, Tenn., that she was then penniless and was on her way to spend the remainder of her days with her son.

Let me ask the fathers and mothers of this land, what else you could expect?

If you desire your sons and daughters to make honorable men and women, have them associate with men and women of honor, and if you think that "Fashionable Summer Resorts" are the places where morality, honor and virtue is found, take them there, but do not complain when you see your children plunge headlong down to despair, shame and misery.

While this chapter is being penned, the Post-Dispatch of St. Louis, Mo., contains the following article:

WEALTHY GIRL'S PLUNGE IN VICE.

SUDDENLY DISAPPEARED ON EVE OF MAR-
RIAGE.

MISSING FOR FIVE DAYS.

RECOGNIZED IN AN INTOXICATED STATE IN
BALTIMORE.

Her Philadelphia Fiance Breaks Engagement, Al-
though Offered Half a Million by Girl's Parents
to Renew It.

"The daughter of one of the wealthiest men in Philadelphia, having a high position in the exclusive circles of the Quaker City, will not be married to the wealthy and socially prominent young man to whom she was engaged.

"Her sudden disappearance some days ago led her parents to believe they had eloped.

"The young man, however, was found in total ignorance of the whereabouts of the missing girl. Five days went by before she was located.

"Then came a letter from Baltimore. The writer was once an intimate friend of the missing girl. She had found her friend on Charles Street, in a pitiable condition of semi-intoxication.

"It was then discovered that the young woman had gone on a 'Bohemian' expedition with a Philadelphia man. A resort in that city was first visited and a day later the couple came to Baltimore.

"They visited a Suburban club where their conduct became so hilarious they were asked to leave. Their whereabouts was then unknown until the following day when the man left the girl.

"That afternoon the young woman, hopelessly intoxicated was seen at a resort with another young man. They were traced to a prominent hotel where the pair registered under the surname of the Philadelphia society man to whom the young woman was to have been married.

"Three days later the recognition occurred on Charles Street, and on the fifth day of her disappearance she returned to her grief-stricken family.

"The young lady's fiance broke off the engagement and an offer is said to have been made to him of half a million dollars to renew it. This he is also reported to have declined."

The Post-Dispatch does not give names, as the wealth of this girl's parents have kept her name from the reporters. However, had this girl have been poor, or did not belong to this gang of "Fashionable Society" her name would have appeared in letters a foot long.

Ten chances to one this girl made her first plunge into shame and immorality from some "Palace of Sin" called "Fashionable Summer Resorts."

Ah, fathers and mothers, look well to the associates of your sons and daughters. If you would have them follow in the footsteps of the good of the land, you must have them associate with men and women of morality, virtue and honor.

WHERE "FASHIONABLE SOCIETY" SPEND THEIR SUNDAYS.

WHERE THE "COMMON PEOPLE" SPEND THEIR SUNDAYS.

THE DIFFERENCE IN MORALS IS EASILY SEEN.

Chapter XIV.

The Awful Spectacle of American Fathers and Mothers Willingly Sacrificing Their Daughters to Foreign Reprobates of Title.

NOBILITY! What does the word mean? Does it mean something noble? Not in the sense we write, by any means, as nobility of foreign lands nearly always means everything that is not noble.

You can not make a NOBLE something out of an ignoble something. Noble manhood is one of the greatest and grandest works of God, but "foreign nobility," in my estimation, and it should be in the estimation of every LIBERTY LOVING man and woman in America, is the most despicable thing on earth.

[231]

"Nobility" when applied to that herd of foreign nonentities generally means an empty-headed "thing" called man, who has no mission on earth but that of pilfering the pockets of toil of its hard-earned sustenance, as "Foreign Nobility" is born into national position, to prey upon manhood, which they claim is their Divine right.

Reader, it is no greater sin for a woman to prostitute her person for money to enable her to gain her livelihood without labor, than it is to prostitute herself for the title that she comes into possession of by marrying into some "Noble" family of foreign birth, and God Almighty will look with as much disfavor, and will pass as awful Judgment upon prostitution of this character as He will upon prostitution in any other form, as it is only the SAME THING in another form.

The most awful spectacle imaginable is to see the rich of this country falling over themselves to offer their daughters to "Foreign Nobility" in order to marry "TITLE," as these foreign reprobates would not think of marrying these girls if they did not know that the parents of the girls were fools, and would lavishly pour out their wealth at their feet.

Oh! how often have I seen girls of wealth hand-

ed over to "titled nobility" as though they were but
so much personal property to be bartered for the
empty and hollow title given some empty-headed
thing by some foreign power.

Now, we would like to analyze "Foreign Nobil
ity" and learn if possible what class of people they
are.

Do we find men of brains and men who by their
own efforts forge to the front and take their place
in the front ranks of men by their individual efforts?
Ah! no; but we find this class of human leaches born
into the position they hold, and it makes no difference whether they are half-witted or not, they become Lords and Princes, just the same as though
they were men of intellect.

Do we find Lords, Princes, Counts, Earls and all
other of these titled nonentities, men of character
and morality? Some few, but the men of character
and morality in this class are the exception and not
the rule.

Did you ever hear of some foreign Prince coming
to this country and marrying a poor girl, no matter
how beautiful she was? Never! they are not looking
for beauty, they are not looking for intellect, they
are not looking for accomplishments; they are not

looking for morality; they are not looking for virtue, but their main object is money. Therefore, they hover about the young women of wealth and these wealthy, old mothers and fathers urge their daughters to prostitute their bodies in order that the family may come in close touch with "nobility" and in order that this daughter of theirs may move in the society of Princes and Princesses.

There is no affection, love nor sentiment connected with a marriage of this kind, as it is purely a proposition of money, the main object being money, on the side of "nobility" and upon the side of these ignorant old Americans, who have more money than brains and less honor than any other one thing they, possess, it is "title" and distinction they are after, therefore, the marriage between "Foreign Nobility" and families of wealth is simply a barter and trade, one side receiving money and the other side receiving "title." The reader will readily see that it is nothing more nor less than a pure case of prostituting the body of the American girl for the sake of royal distinction, which should be and is, a stench in the nostrils of every decent American in the land.

I remember spending three months at Washington, D. C., a number of years ago, becoming ac-

quainted with a sweet-faced girl from New York
State. Her uncle, Philip Mortimer, was a business
man and had made a grand success in this life, as
far as money matters are concerned, as he was worth
I suppose five or six million dollars, and he had an
only daughter, Blanche. This young lady, who I became acquainted with, in after years, when she
learned of my writing a book, told me the story that
I will relate as near as possible, and as this lady
was the niece of the old Millionaire Philip Mortimer,
I think the story is absolutely true.

Blanche had a sweetheart in the State of New
York, who had been at one time her father's private
secretary. This young man was a man of noble character. Now in this sense when we say "noble" we
mean exactly what the word signifies, as Charley
Artwein was a man of morality, of intelligence, and
he was a Christian gentleman, and could be trusted
with anything and everything. This old banker and
manufacturer realized the sterling worth of Charley
Artwein, and he also realized that his daughter
Blanche was in love with Charley, therefore, the outcome of the matter was, that Charley was discharged
from his employ; however, this young man secured
another position that paid him more money and still

pursued his unassuming duties and at the same time
fervently made love to Blanche Mortimer.

He loved this millionaire's daughter with a love
that compromises with nothing and is as steadfast as
the "rock of ages," and each day Blanche Mortimer
learned to love Charley Artwein more tenderly for
his character was above reproach.

Her old father was determined that the match
should be broken off regardless of consequences, as
he was "dead bent" on having his only daughter
marry either wealth or title he was not very particular which, but, as he had wealth to back title, if
there was any preference, he preferred "Foreign Nobility" to wealth, consequently, he turned his business over to his trusted employees and at the beginning of the gay season of Washington, D. C., he took
Blanche and resolved to keep her there until he
weaned her away from Charley Artwein.

He was acquainted with the majority of state-
men, who are at Washington, D. C., during the winter
months, therefore, he and his daughter at once
plunged into Washington society. Of course, Washington society is made up of all classes, and foreign
nobility is largely a part of "Fashionable Society" at
the capital, therefore, Blanche Mortimer came in con-

tact with not only men of national reputation, but with men of wealth and "Foreign Nobility" without end.

Old Mr. Mortimer seemed to forget everything with the exception of his love for notoriety, and his hatred for Charley Artwein, as Blanche refused to be denied the privilege of corresponding with her sweetheart, and absolutely defied her father when he refused to deliver the letters that Charley had written to Blanche,and she informed her father that unless she be allowed not only to receive letters from Charley Artwein, but be permitted to receive her lover when he should call at Washington, that she would elope with him.

Old Mr. Mortimer saw that he had to pursue another course with his daughter, therefore, he told Blanche that if she would wait two years he would give his consent that she marry Charley Artwein. This seemed to greatly please his daughter and with tears in her eyes she threw her arms around her old deceptive father's neck and gave him to understand that he had made her the happiest daughter in the world, as she told him she loved Charley Artwein with a love that could not be conquered, and that she would be miserable all through her natural life if she was not permitted to become his wife.

Her lover was permitted to write as often as he pleased and to call on Blanche as often as he came to the City of Washington. This, however, was not often, as Charley Artwein's duties were so great that he could not get away very often, and he also was ambitious to make money, therefore, did not spend his money in going to the City of Washington very often. However, each day brought a letter to Charley Artwein from Blanche, and she also received a letter from Charley.

The first year since old Mr. Mortimer had given his consent to Charley's and Blanche's marriage had rolled by, and the second year had started and was slipping by fast.

Blanche's father had no intention of allowing them to marry when he promised, but only did it thinking that he could wean Blanche from her "poverty-stricken" lover, as he called him. But such was not the case, for he soon learned that pure love was not so easily frustrated, consequently, old Mr. Mortimer was becoming desperate, as Blanche had already begun to make arrangements for the marriage.

He took Blanche into society and continually kept her in touch with the sons of millionaires and with "titled nobility" and in every conceivable manner endeavored to transfer Blanche's affection from Charley Artwein to any other individual, especially if he possessed either money or "title," but it seemed as though he had utterly failed and the 10th of December was drawing near. This was the date that Charley Artwein and Blanche were to be married.

Charley Artwein's employer was interested in a large factory in the City of New York, and Charley was entrusted with the money twice each month to pay off the employees, consequently, he had to go some twenty squares from the main office to the factory and carry with him from fifteen thousand to twenty-five thousand dollars twice each month.

Old man Mortimer was determined to stop the marriage at all hazard, so it is learned and learned upon good authority, that he hired a detective and instructed him to go down to the Bowery or in any locality in the City of New York and employ some villain to rob Charley Artwein on his way to the factory on a certain Saturday the latter part of October, as this was the busiest season, and he well knew this young clerk would have a large amount of money. In the great City of New York you can hire 'most anything done you want done, and old Philip Mortimer had money at his command, therefore, he em-

(19)

ployed a villain to entice **Charley Artwein** to enter
the factory of his employer from a rear door. This
villain stood at the front door and instructed Charley
Artwein that the front elevator was out of order,
therefore, he would have to go to the back door.
This agent of old man Mortimer was dressed in the
garb of a workingman, and, of course, Charley
thought he had been placed there by the foreman of
the factory, so this villain and young Artwein walked
to the back alley to take the rear elevator.

As they were about to approach the rear door, a
confederate of old man Mortimer's hired villain
snatched the satchel that contained something near
Twenty Thousand Dollars, while the other villain
knocked Charley senseless with a heavy sand bag.
They both escaped with the money, and within a few
moments Charley Artwein staggered into the factory
and informed the foreman that he could not pay off,
as he had been robbed.

The money that these villains had received from
Charley was taken to the boarding house of Charley
Artwein and placed in the mattress of his bed,
in exactly the same packages that his employer had
delivered it to him before he started to the factory.

Charley's employer had absolute confidence in his

integrity and never doubted but what he had been robbed, but old Philip Mortimer had sent a hired detective to Charley's employer, and this detective intimated that Charley Artwein was a very "smooth young fellow" and also intimated that he had heard before that he had done some very questionable things, and further stated that his previous employer, Philip Mortimer, had quietly let Charley go, simply because he had been systematically robbed. Of course, this naturally put Charley's employer to thinking, and while he was loathe to believe that his confidential clerk was anything but an honest gentleman, he concluded to rigidly investigate the matter, thinking that if Charley was straight there would be no harm to make a rigid investigation, and if he was not straight it was time to find it out, as Charley Artwein handled hundreds of thousands of dollars of his employer's money.

As soon as this young clerk sufficiently recovered from the slugging he received, he returned to the office of his employer, and in a straightforward manner told him what had happened, and his employer believed every word he had told him, and Charley remained in his employ without being suspected in the least, but as soon as this detective took his employer to one side and whispered these infamous lies into his ears, of course Charley's actions were closely guarded and an investigation was started at once.

His employer employed this detective, who was also hired by Philip Mortimer, so this detective called upon Charley one morning and told him he would like to have a talk with him in the presence of his employer, and this young man, of course, being absolutely innocent, gladly consented, as he knew there was no guilt that could be attached to him. The detective boldly accused him of being his own robber, and stated that he had planned and executed the game well.

Charley Artwein denied the accusation bitterly and was heart broken, but the detective with old Philip Mortimer's money backing him, boldly declared that he could prove that this confidential clerk had robbed himself. An investigation was started, and the next day Charley's room was searched, and in the bottom of his mattress was found every dollar of the money in the same packages it was in when delivered to this young man to go to the factory and pay the help. Of course, there was no one more surprised than Charley Artwein. However, the detective only declared that it was all assumed, and intimated that he was the "slickest thief" he had ever come in contact with. As to be expected, Charley Artwein was thrown into jail, and no one would go on his bond. Therefore, he was forced to remain there.

Blanche Mortimer, as soon as she heard of her lover's condition, and before she learned the details, rushed to the City of New York to defend the idol of her heart, but as soon as an explanation was made to her that this money was found in Charley Artwein's mattress this girl refused to even go to the jail to see her lover, as she was thoroughly convinced that he was a thief, for her father and this detective had told her that Charley Artwein had been under suspicion before and further stated that he had made this steal to enable him to start in the world with considerable money. All of this talk from her father and the detective had its weight, and Blanche Mortimer learned to hate this innocent young man with as much hatred as she once loved him.

It seemed as though Blanche Mortimer abandoned every thought of Charley Artwein, and no one ever heard her mention his name. Of course, her father painted this innocent young man in the darkest colors imaginable, and told Blanche that she had escaped an awful fate, as she was almost on the eve of marrying a thief.

After that Blanche felt inclined to take her father's advice, in regard to all things, and especially the company whom she had.

Old man Mortimer was afraid that some of his hired tools might go back upon him and divulge this infamous plot, therefore, he conceived the idea of having his daughter marry as soon as possible. Consequently, it was not long until a Spanish nobleman was introduced to Blanche, and her father urged her to give him her undivided attention, which she did, and it was not long until society was notified that during the early part of June Miss Blanche Mortimer was to become the wife of a Spanish nobleman.

Charley Artwein had saved considerable money, as he had always been frugal. Therefore, he employed two first-class lawyers to defend him, but no sooner would he employ a lawyer than Philip Mortimer would buy him off, as he did not want first-class legal talent employed to defend Charley, knowing full well that as soon as the case was sifted, as first-class lawyers would do, that his scheme was in danger of being laid bare. Therefore, as soon as an at-

torney was employed by Charley, this lawyer would
be taken dangerously ill or at least would claim to
be sick, and, of course, Charley was left without an
attorney.

It is stated that this young man employed no less
than twelve or fourteen attorneys, who invariably
put up some excuse why they could not defend him,
and it is learned upon good authority that Philip
Mortimer paid out thousands upon thousands of dollars in order to keep him from being represented by
first-class talent.

This young man had to be content and put up
with inferior lawyers. It is said that even those poor
lawyers whom Charley employed were paid a large
sum of money by this detective, but furnished by
Mortimer to make their defense as light as possible
so as to make conviction doubly certain.

This young man wrote letter after letter to
Blanche Mortimer, and explained to her that he was
as innocent of the crime that he was accused of as
an unborn babe, but not a word did he receive from
the girl whom he loved better than he loved his own
soul.

It is also stated that this same detective that was
hired by Philip Mortimer visited Charley Artwein in

his cell, and offered him Twenty-five Thousand Dollars if he would leave the City, and also agreed to furnish him a bondsman in the sum of Ten Thousand Dollars, stating that the bondsman would make good the bond after he had disappeared. He explained the matter to Charley by stating, that he was a young man who had business ability and that his employer did not want to blast his future. But when this offer was made, Charley Artwein became furious with rage and informed this detective, hired by Mortimer's millions that he would rather go to the penitentiary for life than to proclaim to the world that he was guilty, and his leaving the city would be equivalent to acknowledging his guilt.

It seems as though old man Mortimer's conscience was pricking him ,as away down in his heart he knew Charley was as honorable a man as ever lived, therefore, he was anxious to in some manner protect Charley from his sure fate, so he resorted to this plan of giving him Twenty-five Thousand Dollars and furnishing a bondsman for him, but he failed in his undertaking, as this young man's honor was not to be bought with the paltry sum of Twenty-five Thousand Dollars. In fact, there had never been enough money minted to cause Charley Artwein to acknowledge that he was a thief.

When this scheme would not work, this detective informed this young man that Blanche Mortimer was to be married in June, thinking that Charley would become desperate and gladly accept the Twenty-five Thousand Dollars and leave the country.

Old man Mortimer had reasoned that as soon as Charley learned that he had lost Blanche that he would become desperate and gladly accept these terms, so the detective explained to him that there was no use of him fighting the case, as he would be convicted, and even should he be cleared he had nothing to gain, as Blanche Mortimer would be married before his trial could come off. But this young man declared that if he lost the idol of his heart that he would still retain his character, and stoutly refused to compromise and demanded naught but justice, thinking that it was an absolute impossibility for him to be convicted of such a dastardly crime that he was not guilty of committing. However, he was not acquainted with the abominable ways of wealth and "Fashionable Society," as this class of people does not stop short of anything to accomplish their ends, no matter what it is nor who suffers by their actions.

Blanche Mortimer was to be married on the 2nd

day of June to this Spanish "nonentity" who claimed
to possess royal blood, but he was nothing more nor
less than a reprobate and the only thing that he held
out to old man Mortimer and his daughter was his
Noble (?) Birth.

Charley's trial was set for the 3rd day of May,
and his lawyers, to more impress their client that
they were doing their best, had the trial postponed
until the first day of the following month, which was
the 1st day of June, and which was also one day before Blanche Mortimer was to be married to this
Spaniard. However, it turned out to be a God-send
to Charley, as the postponing of his trial saved him
from conviction.

It seemed as though old man Mortimer's detective
had endeavored to force this old millionaire to pay
him a large sum of money above the stipulated price
to convict Charley Artwein. This, it seemed, the old
rascal stoutly refused to do, telling the detective
that he had given him a big price for his work, and
informing him that a "contract was a contract," and
he did not propose to give him any more money, also
stating that it had already cost him a great deal
more than he had figured on.

The latter part of May this detective, whose name

was Andy Milan, went to the old man and told him
unless he was paid a quarter of a million dollars between then and 10 o'clock the 1st day of June, which
was the day of Charley Artwein's trial, he would
go on the witness stand and swear it was a "set up
job," and that he was paid so much money to convict this young man, who was as innocent as an
angel in Heaven.

Old Philip Mortimer believed that this was only
a bluff and told Andy Milan to do as he pleased
about it, but that he had received every penny from
him that he would get. This detective made the
second threat, but to no avail, as old man Mortimer
was thoroughly convinced in his own mind that it
was only a bluff. but he had not considered the desperate character of this hired detective, as a man
of this character will do anything to accomplish his
end. However, this old millionaire would not budge
an inch. On the last day of May, which was the day
before Charley Artwein's trial was to come off, and
two days before Blanche Mortimer was to be married,
Andy Milan rang the door bell of this old millionaire's mansion and inquired for Blanche Mortimer,
stating that he had an important message that could
only be delivered to her in person.

The maid informed this detective that she would convey the message to her Mistress, but Andy Milan with the desperation of a desperate man informed her that under no circumstances could he deliver his message except to Blanche Mortimer in person, consequently, this young lady appeared at the door and Andy Milan in a cool and deliberate manner says, "Young lady, were you ever acquainted with a young man by the name of Charles Artwein?" She, of course, informed him that she had been, and this detective then asked her where he was? And she told him in jail, in the City of New York, awaiting his trial for theft and when he received his just deserts he would spend the remainder of his life, or a good portion of it in the penitentiary.

This detective says, "Young lady, I am personally acquaintetd with Chas. Artwein, who is as innocent of the crime that he is accused of as you, and a thousand times more innocent than your old father, who was the instigator of this plot, which would enable him to blast the hopes of this noble young man in order that you might marry a man of wealth or a man of noble birth."

Blanche Mortimer's lips quivered for a few moments, but only for a few moments, for she soon regained her composure, and said: "Will you repeat to my father what you have repeated to me?"

The detective simply replied, "Yes."

In a moment old Philip Mortimer came down the hall in his silken smoking jacket, his daughter having informed him that some one at the door desired to see him, but did not tell him who it was. This old scheming villain had no idea who it was until he reached the door. Then he did not recognize in this man Andy Milan, as this detective in the few seconds that Blanche had been gone had slipped on a false beard, which completely disguised him.

When this old millionaire reached the door, he simply said, "Who are you?"

The detective in a deliberate manner said "Andy Milan." The old gentleman turned as pale as death and says, "You are not, or if you are you are not the Andy Milan I know."

By this time Blanche had reached the side of her father and says "If this is not the Andy Milan you know, pray tell me what kind of a looking man he is?"

Her father snorted that this was none of her business, and ordered her to return to her room.

At this time the detective slipped off his false

beard and asked Mr. Mortimer if he then knew him.

Old Philip Mortimer threw up his hands and exclaimed, "What do you want here, you scoundrel?"

"Oh, nothing," replied the detective, "as I have performed my mission, but I just waited to see you because your daughter wanted me to."

The old millionaire clutched the side of the door and gasped "Go to my office at once, and I will meet you there in twenty minutes, and will pay you the money you ask."

The detective simply remarked, "Oh, you have been too slow, as I have already told your daughter that Charley Artwein never stole a penny from his employer, and that you were the guilty one."

One would suppose that this girl would have fainted at such a statement, but instead of that she rang for a servant and sent a dispatch to Chas. Artwein, who was in jail in the City of New York, stating that she would be at his trial on the following day.

She addressed another message to the royal Spaniard, to whom she was to be married on June the second, stating that the marriage would not come off, also stating that she would leave the city within an hour.

Blanche Mortimer took the train that evening for the City of New York, and called at the jail and informed Chas. Artwein that she would be at his trial and for him to take courage, stating that she would defend him with every dollar that her father possessed.

This young man knew nothing of what had transpired between the detective and the Mortimer family, but he was the happiest man that ever stood behind the bars of a prison cell.

The next morning before the trial began old Philip Mortimer had arrived in the City of New York and had gone to Charley Atwein's cell, and had offered him a fabulous amount of money to leave the city, stating that he would give bond for his appearance in court, and would see that the bond was paid, but to this proposition the young man only replied: "If you possessed every dollar in the world you could not induce me to leave the City of New York, for by leaving I would brand myself as a thief, and Mr. Mortimer, you know as well as I do, that I am as innocent of the crime that I am accused of as you are yourself."

Charles Artwein had never dreamed that this old scheming villain was the cause of his downfall, so he did not brand the old millionaire as being the conspirator of his miseries.

When Philip Mortimer found that he could not bribe Charley to leave the city, he then went to the young man's employer and proposed to give Charley's employer Fifty Thousand Dollars if he would not appear against Artwein at his trial, but Charley's previous employer had as much money as old man Mortimer, therefore, he could not be induced not to appear against the young man. Charley's employer told Mr. Mortimer that it would be compounding a crime by failing to appear and prosecute a thief. Therefore, he utterly refused to do so.

To delay the trial Philip Mortimer went to Charley's lawyers and had them ask for a continuance, which they did, and the trial was set off until the 20th of June.

Mortimer reasoned that if he could get the trial postponed that he could in the meantime, by some hook or crook, and with his vast amount of wealth, keep it from ever coming to trial, and in some manner hush the matter up, as it had gone so far that he would have given all his wealth could he have undone what he had done.

It had been an impossibility for Charley Artwein

to furnish a bondsman, but when the trial was postponed old Philip Mortimer walked up to the Judge and proposed to go on the young man's bond. Of course, he was accepted, as he was known to be a man possessing many millions.

Blanche Mortimer was in the courtroom on the morning the trial was to take place, and when her father arose and proposed to go on the bond of Charley Artwein, she burst into tears and frantically threw her arms about her father's ungodly neck.

Blanche had not spoken to Charley Artwein that morning, but as soon as the bond was made out, and old Philip Mortimer had signed it and Charley Artwein had started to leave the courtroom a free man for at least a short time, Blanche Mortimer rushed down the aisle and in a frantic manner rained kiss upon kiss upon the brow of this young man who had been confined to his cell for a number of months.

It is stated that Philip Mortimer looked upon this scene with tears streaming down his face, and when Artwein and Blanche walked hand in hand out of the court house door, this old millionaire followed them and overtook them and told Charley Artwein that he would spend every dollar that he possessed to clear him.

(20)

About this time Andy Milan again made his appearance upon the scene and informed Philip Mortimer that if he proposed to bring this trial to such a sudden close that he had to pay for it, as he did not intend for him to escape a just penalty for his villany in the matter, unless he (Andy Milan) was paid for it.

So he renewed his demand for a quarter of a million dollars, and agreed that if he should receive this amount of money he would immediately leave America.

Old Mr. Mortimer gave him the money, and Andy Milan, I am informed, went to Australia and stayed there a number of years, but broke his contract and eventually came back to the City of New York, broken in health, where he died a few years afterwards.

On the 20th of June, the case of Charles Artwein was again called and was again postponed by request of the defense, as old Philip Mortimer could not persuade the prosecuting witness not to appear against him.

This old millionaire did not desire to inform Charley's employer that he was at the bottom of this villainous plot to deprive the young man of his liberty. Therefore, he exhausted all of his ingenuity in endeavoring to accomplish his end by some other means, but it seemed as though it was an impossibility.

Just before Artwein's trial was called for the fourth time, old man Mortimer arrived at the conclusion that there was no other way out of the dilemma, but for him to go direct to Charley's employer and openly acknowledge that he had hired the detective to rob Charley, and also had hired the detective to place the money in Artwein's mattress, and frankly tell him that he had done this in order to prevent his daughter Blanche from marrying this young man, as he was anxious for his daughter to marry a man of wealth, or a man possessing a "title."

It is stated that Philip Mortimer actually got down upon his knees to Charley's previous employer and, with tears in his eyes, made the confession and begged him not to appear as the prosecuting witness and told him if he would not, he would give his consent for Blanche to marry Charley, and he would help them in every conceivable manner.

After this explanation, and with a good round lecture from Charley's previous employer, he agreed not to prosecute the young man, and further agreed to never divulge Philip Mortimer's secret.

This old millionaire went at once to Blanche and
told her what he had done, which seemed to very
much delight this heartbroken girl.

In the meantime, however, Charley had learned
that this old villain was the cause of his arrest and,
of course, he naturally despised him. However, he covered up his dislike as much as
possible in order not to offend Blanche, for,
of course, while Blanche knew that her father had
performed this most dastardly act, Charley realized
that he was her father, and she could not but love
him.

As soon as Mr. Mortimer told Blanche what he
had accomplished, this girl at once went to Charley
and informed him what had transpired, but Charles
Artwein was not the kind of a man to rest under a
cloud. Therefore, he demanded that he should go to
trial, as he proposed to have every shadow of his
guilt removed from his character. This, of course,
placed the matter in a different light, but it only increased Blanche's love for Charley, for she saw that
his stand was right. Therefore, another great ob-
stacle confronted the old millionaire, as Charles demanded that every vestige of guilt be removed from
his character, and this could not be done without a
trial and an acquittal, and the only way that Philip

Mortimer could see how he could be acquitted was by
he himself declaring in open court that he was the
instigator of Charley Artwein's arrest, which he did
not want to do.

The reader will remember that Andy Milan had
a confederate, who helped to rob Charley and place
the money in his mattress, so just about the time
that Philip Mortimer was in this great dilemma, this
confederate of Andy Milan appeared at the office of
the millionaire and demanded Ten Thousand Dollars,
stating that if he did not receive it, he would divulge the part that the old millionaire had played in
the arrest of this young man.

At once Mr. Mortimer conceived the idea of
hiring this villain to make oath that he had robbed
Charley and for fear of detection had hid the money
in the mattress, in order to convict this trusted em-
ploye and remove any possible probability of conviction from him. This confederate of Andy Milan had
boarded at the same boarding house that Charles
Artwein had. This was a part of the game
for this confederate to board with the young man and
to learn as much as possible about his business, so
that they would be prepared to intercept the young
man at the proper time when he was going to the
factory to pay the help.

The old millionaire told this confederate that he would give him Twenty-five Thousand Dollars if he would go on the stand and make oath that he had robbed Artwein and further stated that he would do his utmost with the court to have his sentence cut down to the least possible penalty.

This villain who had caused Charley Artwein so much trouble and distress of mind concluded he would do so, provided he would not get over five years in the penitentiary for his offense, and old Mr. Mortimer informed him that he would do his best to get his penalty cut down to two years if possible.

So the morning of the trial Benj. Anant arose from his seat and addressed the court, and stated that he was the man who had robbed Charles Artwein at the factory last October. He went into detail and described the circumstances so minutely that the court was convinced of his statement, and informed Charles Artwein that he was released from custody. Anant's attorney asked the court to suspend judgment for a few days and in the meantime the attorneys and Philip Mortimer went to the Judge and had him to place the penalty at two years. This, dear reader, is the first time in history this diabolical deed has been told to the world. However, there were two or three outside of the detectives and Charley Artwein and Blanche who knew of Philip Mortimer's awful crime.

Within a few days Charley Artwein received a letter from his previous employer, who proposed to reinstate him in the position he held at the time the robbery had occurred, but this young man thanked him cordially, for his offer, but told him that he did not care to be associated with the same men that he had been before this awful crime was committed. Artwein's employer informed him that he was sorry he had ever promised Philip Mortimer that he would not divulge the part that he had played in Artwein's downfall, and stated that he felt that Philip Mortimer should go to the penitentiary and suffer for the awful sin he had committed, but he had promised not to divulge it, therefore, the secret remained with him.

Blanche Mortimer had learned to love Charley Artwein again with a devotion that was akin to worship, as all of her old love had returned and had been multiplied many, many times by the awful injustice that had been done her lover.

Charles Artwein informed Blanche that he thought the best thing for them to do was to separate as friends, but informed her that he would love her as long as there was life in his body, to which Blanche replied that she was ready and would only be too glad to become his wife.

Charles Artwein, with a hatred in his heart that could scarcely be described, went to old Mr. Mortimer and told him that he loved Blanche, but did not feel as though he should marry her without his consent. However, he did not believe that he had any right to dictate to him or Blanche in regard to their future happiness. The old gentleman broke down and wept like a child, and told this young man that he would deem it a great honor to have him as his son-in-law.

The day was set for the marriage, and Blanche wrote her Spanish fiance that the engagement between them must be broken, and further stated that she had never loved him as a woman should love a man before she married him.

On the 10th of December following, Blanche Mortimer became the wife of Charley Artwein, and this young man to-day is a power in the business world in the City of Chicago, for he and his young bride left New York immediately after they married. His old father-in-law lavishly poured his wealth at Charley's feet, but it was refused with many thanks, as Charley Artwein informed his father-in-law that he felt capable and competent of making his way in the world without any assistance.

He entered the employ of a "packing house" in Chicago, and rapidly forged to the front, and he is to-day the heaviest stockholder in one of the largest packing concerns in America.

Blanche's father died within less than a year after Blanche was married.

His niece informed me that she believed his death was caused by remorse, as he never afterwards appeared to be the same man.

Of course, at the old man's death, Blanche fell heir to all of his wealth, which amounted to several millions of dollars, as Blanche was the only child.

Blanche's mother had died when she was only a child, therefore, she never knew the tender care and affection of a mother's love.

The Spaniard that Blanche was to marry remained in Washington, D. C., for several months, and finally married the daughter of another millionaire. It is a certain fact that he lavishly squandered this girl's money, and deserted her after returning to Madrid, Spain.

After this Spaniard, who boasted of belonging to the "titled" family of Spain, squandered his wife's money, he treated her so shamefully that she was compelled to return to America penniless, as her parents had died, and their wealth had been squandered by the daughter's noble (?) husband.

This is the dark-skinned devil, whom old Philip Mortimer endeavored to force his daughter to marry, and almost wrecked the life of Charles Artwein to accomplish his end.

If it was not for the misery brought upon the innocent children of such marriages, one could not pity the silly girls who so willingly are led to the altar by these noble (?) devils, who are seeking our American heiresses, not for wives, but for the money they come into possession of by marrying them.

We do not have to ransack history for parallel cases with Blanche Mortimer and Charles Artwein as we can go to the city of New York, or any other large city, for that matter, and find wealthy families who have willingly stood by and seen their daughters prostitute their bodies to foreign nobility to become wives in name only, for those foreigners who boast their "title" and their "noble birth" are in a great majority of cases void of honor and manhood, and only come to this country to regain a fortune which they have perhaps lost in "riotous living."

"Oh! for a thousand tongues" to proclaim to the world the abominations of "Fashionable Society."

Reader, you must bear in mind that this book only contains a small part of what I have witnessed and heard from others who have tramped down this filthy road of "society," as it would be impossible for me to put into print and circulate the darkest acts of this unholy tribe.

Philip Mortimer was willing to sink his soul into hell to have his own daughter, his own blood and flesh, become the wife of one of these Noble (?) Devils, which is in my estimation the lowest class of men that ever infested the face of the earth.

I would to God that the mothers and fathers of this land actually knew what "Fashionable Society" really means as it is a task that no one can do justice to, for you can not give the facts in all of their awfulness.

Charley Artwein and Blanche are still living in the City of Chicago, and while they are worth millions in their own name, regardless of what was left them by Blanche's father, they have never permitted this "Hag of Society" to darken their door and their children have never been permitted to enter that slippery path of "Fashionable Society." Blanche's cousin informed me that both Mr. Artwein and his wife consider that "Fashionable Society" is responsible for what so nearly wrecked their happiness.

Once in a great while you find men of wealth who are men of honor, but most generally they have learned a bitter lesson by having come in contact at some time with this "She Devil" of society, or by having some of their children crushed by the slime and pollution that continually drips from the filthy sewer in "high life."

When our preachers learn that they can not deliver sermons gotten up especially for the rich and serve God ε. the same time, it is then that they will reach out .nd awake the souls and minds of the nation, and place a new song upon our lips and lift the "common people" to a higher plane of life. But just so long as our preachers cater to those who pay them the most money, just that long will the arrogance of wealth and the contamination of "Fashionable Society" wield an influence over the morals of this country that will pull down the hopes of mothers and the ambitions of fathers and destroy the prospects of sons and blacken the characters of our daughters.

"ENVY" — We envy those who despise themselves.

Chapter XV.

***

The Sin of Wanting to be What We are not, and What We Cannot Afford to be.

***

How many homes have been wrecked by the inmates desiring to be what they are not, and longing to be just what their neighbors look to be.

The women, God bless them, are prone to be dissatisfied with their lot in life, as they behold the "finery" of thir neighbors and become dissatisfied with their own clothes. They see the splendid carriages and matched teams their neighbors drive, and at once the Devil plants the seed of discontent in their hearts, and they either become envious or dissatisfied with their own surroundings, and dissatisfaction with your own surroundings is equivalent to being en-

vious, and I can not think of a more miserable word
in the English language than "envy."

You see your neighbors with their fine clothes, fine
jewelry, fine furniture, fine horses and rigs, and you
at once begin to compare your surroundings with
theirs. You say, "I work just as hard as Mrs. So-and-
So, and my children are just as smart and good
looking as hers, but still I can't have all the elegant
things that she and her children have."

You let your children know you are dissatisfied,
and it is not long until you have them brooding over
their "hard lot."

You plant the seed of "envy" in their hearts, and
by your everlasting complaining and comparisons, you
soon have a full grown weed of "envy" developed, to
plague that child during the remainder of its days.

By your own acts you have made the life of your
husband miserable, as he begins to notice that his
children do not dress as well as those of his neighbors'.

What is the result? He either loses heart in his
business, or makes a vow that his family shall dress
as well as his neighbor's and makes one great effort
and fails, and then with another resolve born of desperation he becomes a defaulter and robs his employ-

er, or makes an assignment if he is in business for himself, as he has learned too late that the demands of his wife and children are too great for his once prosperous little business to sustain.

You do not stop to investigate and learn whether this family with their fine clothes and elegant "turn out" can afford it or not. You do not know that perhaps they "stint their stomachs" in order to appear in the eyes of their neighbors to be what they are not.

You do not know whether that family is happy with all of their fine equipage or not. You do not know how many sleepless nights that father has spent in racking his brain to devise some way by which he may pay his obligations that his neighbors may not learn of his financial embarrassments.

It is a well known fact that some of the most magnificent oaks that adorn the forests have "wind-shaken" hearts, and so it is with at least one-half of the families who make a great show, their interior is all at fault.

Your wife and children have all the necessities of life that go to make home happy, as fine clothes, elegant carrigaes and high stepping horses do not make happiness.

(21)

Your children sit down to a table well laden with wholesome food, while perhaps the children of your neighbors who display their elegance and would impress you with their financial worth have a very meagre diet, for that mother who thinks more of impressing her neighbors with her great importance has to "cut expenses" somewhere in order to do so, therefore she begins at the table and goes right on down the line and "cuts expenses" everywhere, only so far as it would not affect outward appearances.

Does what your neighbors think of you add anything to what you actually are?

Does your neighbor dressing in elegance and sustaining a stable of fine horses and a beautiful carriage, work any hardship upon you?

"HONOR" is the rockribbed essential that you must have in order that you may know within your own heart that you are men and women, and no outward demonstration can convince you of this fact as this inborn knowledge must come by and through your own acts, therefore why need you "envy" that which your neighbor possesses and which does not add a hair's breadth to your stature or detract a particle from your manhood or womanhood.

Our miseries generally come from this innocent-

looking little word "envy" for we behold our neighbor
with something that we do not possess, and we at once
have a desire to have something "just as good" or
better. In fact, we always try to go a little farther
than our neighbor has gone, as we are not even satisfied to be his equal in appearance, but we want to
impress him and our other neighbors that we are better, if anything. What is the result?

The result is simply this, that we tax our finances
to a point where it becomes dangerous and it places
us in "hot water" as it were, to meet our obligations,
as they fall due, and when we have once entered this
silly practice, it is a great deal harder to stop it
and "cut down expenses" than it would have been to
have done without in the first place all of these things
which does not add a moment's happiness to our
lives nor does not raise us an inch in the estimation
of our friends, for as soon as our friends and neighbors
realize that we are going beyond what they consider
our means, they at once consider us either extravagant
or fools, therefore they lose their respect for us. You
have not only lost the respect of your neighbors and
friends who moved in the same circle that you once
did, but you have caused those you patterned after
to despise you, because they have to make another
sacrifice to "outshine" you.

There are hundreds of mothers in this land who are satisfied with their dress until they see some one else with a better one, or at least one they think looks better, when at once they make themselves miserable by allowing this little word "envy" to assert itself. They are satisfied with their surroundings until they know of their neighbor's children having some garment that was bought in some "great city," when at once this poor old simple mother becomes dissatisfied with the clothes of her children, simply because they were bought at the "neighboring store."

What does this all lead to? Ah! nothing more nor less than a "Fashionable Society" right in the midst of the "common people," however, this "Fashionable Society" in the neighborhood is confined to the desire to "outshine" their neighbors in clothes, and has not yet reached the degrading stage of immorality, but we shade our eyes and look right down the line and we see these "country folks" establishing in a small way, a "Fashionable Society" within their midst that develops gradually into "Fashionable Society" of wealth, immorality and degradation.

Be it said to the ever-lasting honor and credit of the "common people" that you do not find so many envious individuals as you do among the wealthy, but the principle is as despicable among the poor as it is among the rich.

I knew a family in my boyhood who lived in the southern part of Indiana that was the "envy" of at least one-half of the neighbors and the other half endeavored to pattern after this family, as far as their clothes were concerned, however, be it said to the credit of this neighborhood they did not endeavor to follow their example as far as morals were concerned.

We will call this family by the name of Sharper for convenience sake. The father was a man who was very unscrupulous in regard to how he made his money, as everything was "grist" that came to his mill.

He owned a large farm and in addition to the revenues he derived from his farm he was interested in another business from which he made considerable money. The ambition of this family was to "out-dress" and "outshine" all of their neighbors in every particular. They had no regard for God and his laws, therefore, of course, did not respect the laws of man to any great extent, and no further than was absolutely necessary to protect them from its clutches.

They had a number of both sons and daughters, and their ambition was to make their neighbors feel as small as possible when in their presence.

I am now speaking in a general way regarding this family, as one of the sons was several degrees higher in the scale of manhood than the majority of the children, however, he has never written his name exceedingly high on the "Tablet of Fame" in the profession which he follows.

This family had what could be termed a country mansion, elegantly furnished, fine horses and carriages without number.

Their father was a man of more than average intelligence, but he only used h s intell. t tc get advantage of his fellow man and regarded his fellow man as only a "something" that he considered was his privilege to oppress, and he never missed an opportunity to oppress.

A man who does not respect the laws of God can not respect the laws of man, only so far as it is to his advantage to do so, therefore if he does not respect the laws of God and man, it is unreasonable to suppose that he possesses the finer feelings and nobler principles of man, consequently the reader will not be surprised to learn that he shamefully mistreated his own father, and a man or woman who will treat unkindly the father and mother who brought them into this world and cared for them when they could not

care for themselves, is not deserving to be called
"MAN."

From all outward indications one would suppose
that this family with their elegance and seemingly
every desire being granted, would live in happiness,
but such was not the case, as there was a continual
turmoil and dissatisfaction among the children, and
you could expect nothing else, for when their father
before them had turned from his door his old white-
haired father, bent with years, upon the charity of
his neighbors what could you expect of his children?

This family treated their neighbors as though
they were created for their special benefit, conse-
quntly, of course, they were despised by the majority
of the neighbors, however, these same neighbors
would envy the Sharpers for their fine clothes and
elegant "turn outs."

However, there came a day when prosperity seemed to turn to ashes of despair, and the black vulture
of shame perched herself over this country mansion.

The father died. The children as well as the mother lawed among themselves, for the pittance the
father had left, which was a very small amount, as his
wonderful wealth in the imagination of the neighbors,
had dwindled down to a very few thousand, and this

amount was partially squandered in lawyers' fees and court costs by litigation among the children and mother.

Financial troubles could have been endured, but scandal after scandal attached itself to the members of this family, and today no family in that section is thought so little of as the one I write about, and no family in that neighborhood has as few followers.

The arrogance of their past actions only served as a hideous nightmare to haunt their present, and their future will be a desolate waste, strewn with bitter remembrances of the past.

This is the family that mothers once envied.

This is the family that caused discontent in the minds of the neighbors and their children. This is the family that fathers and mothers were envious of because they and their children could not wear as fine clothes and afford as fine "turnouts" as this Sharper family, but today the poorest family in that section holds up this Sharper family as a warning to their children and tells them of the arrogance that this family once possessed, but who has now been humbled in the dust, which is certain to follow in the wake of dishonest and unscrupulous transactions.

Contentment is more to be sought after than

wealth, as the mind that is content with its surroundings, provided the individual has endeavored to make use of its God-given ability, is as near perfection as is possible in this life.

Ambition and contentment are two separate and distinct words. Ambition means a desire for greater things and contentment means, at ease, or a satisfied feeling, with present surroundings.

You may say that if you are ambitious that you can not be contented, but such is not the case, for if your ambition is a righteous ambition, it will be content and satisfied with your best efforts, and no man or woman can please God without putting forth their best efforts, which means satisfaction to your conscience, for whenever we fail to do our best, our conscience pricks us.

It would be just as reasonable for all of us to eLvy the great orator, the great singer, the great musician, or the great preacher, as it would for us to envy the man or woman who chances to wear better clothes than we do.

Do you suppose that the crow with his raven wings envies the tropical bird with its brilliant plumage? NEVER! The crow is content with the color of his dress!

Do you suppose that the eagle with his mighty scream which does not contain a single melodious note, envies the Nightingale, as she pours forth her beautiful melody? Never! That old eagle is proud of her harsh voice, and not one thought of envy does she bestow upon the sweet singer of the night.

Do you suppose that the nimble-footed deer of the forest envies the powerful ox his strength? Never! She is content with her meekness and agility.

Do you suppose the little star that glitters in the heavens looks with envy upon the moon in all of her glory? Never! The star has a mission to fill and does not for a moment envy the moon her magnificent splendor.

Contentment, then, is not only an indication of wisdom, but it is a duty that you owe God to be content with what your lot is, provided, however, that you have not, by some act of your own, made your lot a miserable one.

Contentment is the blessed assurance of having performed your duty, and both men and women know full well when they have righteously performed their duty, as that little thing, called "conscience" is nothing more nor less than the whisperings of an omnipotent God, which tells us when we have, or have not, performed that duty.

Oh! if the mothers and fathers of this land would banish from their minds every thought of covetousness, which is only another name for "envy," what happy homes we would have throughout the breadth and length of this land.

Let your neighbors wear silks if they like, but before you undertake to dress yourself and family in these expensive garments ask yourself, "Can I afford to do it?"

Wives and children, before you make your husbands and fathers miserable by your requests, first ask yourself, "Can our husbands and fathers afford it?"

Remember that while you are sitting in your little home envious of your neighbors' finery and their carriages and horses, that perhaps that awful weight of "debt" which is a nightmare and a hideous dream to any right thinking man or woman, may be weighing this family down and keeping their nose to the "grind stone" as it were, in order to make this outward appearance.

Ah! I would rather have the white winged dove of contentment to hover over my thatched roof and be able to look the world in the face and know that I owe no man a single penny, than to have the raiment

of kings and queens and the equipage of oriental
princes, than have my visions by day, and my dreams
by night marred by that awful word "debt."

Reader, I hope this chapter does not fit you, but if
it does, from this time forward make a resolve that
never again will you be discontent with your surroundings, provided that you have done your best.
Whenever you arrive at this conclusion your neighbors' children dressed in silks and satins will not
disturb you in the least. There is an old saying that
"Fine feathers make fine birds," but there was never
a more erroneous statement uttered, as the feathers
are no part of the bird.

Fine raiment may make fine look'ng ladies and
gentlemen, but what is it that const tutes a lady or
a gentleman? Is it their garments? If it is then we
could dress up the most villainous criminal that ever
went unhung, in broad cloth, with patent leather
shoes, a silk hat, and place a two-caret diamond in
his shirt front, and instead of having a criminal, whose
hands are red with the blood of his fellow man, we
would have a "gentleman."

If the garments that we wear make ladies and
gentlemen, we could take the degraded harlot from the
brothel, and dress her in silks and satin and immed-

iately transform her into the noblest work of God "a pure woman."

When we learn that "envy" and covetousness" is the Devil's pet mode of leading mankind to the plains of misery, and that these two words—"envy" and "covetousness"—do not find lodgment in the minds of true men and women and in the minds of men and women of brains, then, and not until then, will we realize that the most beautiful word in the English language is "contentment."